THE HEAVIEST OF BURDENS

MORTALITY BITES SERIES

RAMY VANCE

KEEP EVOLVING STUDIOS

THE HEAVIEST OF BURDENS

A BEGINNING OF SORTS

Our timing needed to be perfect.

Not only did we need to get everyone out before the security alarms started ringing, but we had to do it without being noticed. Which meant that we had just under three minutes to hack into the systems and shut it off.

If we got noticed, then we were dead.

If it took longer than three minutes, then we were dead.

When the gods left, it was calculated that the Others had less than a minute to pack up their shit and get out. Most of them got out in time.

Most.

And we had three whole minutes. Plenty of time, right?

Then again, they didn't need to deal with Memnock Securities and double authentication passwords.

A guard came around the corner just as expected. I kicked him in the chin before putting him in a sleeper hold. Anyone who's ever done one of those would tell you they are an absolute waste of time. It takes minutes for someone to go under, and even then, they wind up waking up in a minute or two.

Good thing the hold was only mean to *hold*. Egya came up behind me and injected the poor guy with something a little bit more permanent. "He'll wake up in about three days with one hell of headache," Egya said as he plunged the syringe into the guard's neck.

Egya wasn't wearing a shirt, and coarse tufts of brown-and-black fur lined his chest like armor. About six months ago, Egya was reminded how to shift back to his hyena form without magic, but he couldn't quite make the full transformation, settling on this hybrid—boy-slash-hyena form.

I was OK seeing my friend with an elongated nose and claw-like hands. But the chest hair ... yu-uk.

"What?" Egya said as he called over a dwarf who grabbed the limp guard and dragged him over.

"You sure these guys are solid?"

"Yes," Egya said. "I vetted each one of them. They'll take the unconscious guards to the quarry near the docks. They're even leaving behind bottled water and a snack for these guys when they wake up. Oh, and a map."

"A map?"

"They're taking them way out. They'll need it to get home."

"Oh, OK." I nodded, not able to take my eyes off his hairy chest.

"Again, what?"

"I know you're relishing these new transformation powers of yours, but can't you wear a shirt?"

He ran his hands through the bristled fur. "What? You no likey?"

"I no likey," I said, and leaned in to give him a big fat kiss on his canine-elongated mouth. "But me toleratey because, overall, the package isn't bad."

Egya pulled me in close for another kiss, but I put a hand up to stop him. "If we survive this—and I'm not sure either of us will—then ..." I said, presenting myself in a Vanna White-style presentation. "But for now, let's keep our heads and hormones in the game. How many guards are left?"

"None."

"Time?"

Egya checked his watch. "Two minutes and change, then the alarms go all klaxon-style on us."

I looked down the hall with frustration. "So where the hell is she?"

"She'll be here," Egya said.

"And you're so sure because she's reliable. You know, in that faithful kind of way?"

Egya rolled his eyes. "She an encantado. Stealing boyfriends is a socially acceptable pastime."

"I know," I said, groaning. It had been a week since I saw her kissing my boyfriend ... my *ex*-boyfriend, and it still stung even though I was over him. I had a new man.

A good one, too, I thought, looking at my grossly hairy new boyfriend. *When he's all man and not half whatever that was.*

"Darling, I'm all man all the time." He smirked.

"Thinking out loud again," I muttered.

Egya nodded.

"One day I'll get a handle on my quirk. One day. Until then—" I cut my own words off when I heard footsteps, as a figure rounded the corner.

In the darkness, I couldn't see if it was her, but Egya's hyena-like eyes were adept at seeing in the dark. *Hunting* in the dark. "It's her," he said, before narrowing his eyes. "Actually, it's you."

As the figure got closer, I saw a woman that was my age, height, hair color, wearing the same tartan I typically wore on one of my vigilante nights out.

She was pretty. Gorgeous, actually. And I'm not saying that because she looked exactly like me.

I'm one hot enchilada, and I know it.

But she wasn't me. She was the encantado shapeshifter who had taken my form ... and I'd never been so relieved to see, well, myself.

1

BOYFRIENDS, BRAZILIANS AND KAT FIGHTS

*Y*ou know how when you've had a long day, all you want to do is snuggle up under your blankets with a good book, a bucket of chocolate, a bottle of wine and your boyfriend?

Well, I've had six months of long days that ended with an even longer stint in the hospital. So when I finally managed to return to Montreal, I figured I'd find Justin and snuggle.

The last thing I wanted was to see him battling a flock of souped-up birds while macking on another woman.

I stared in disbelief as Justin shot arrow after arrow like he was William Friggin' Tell. He was awesome. Too awesome.

I rubbed my eyes in disbelief. I had been gone for a few weeks and maybe, just maybe, I wasn't witnessing what I was witnessing. It could be an illusion, or my concussion being more serious than what the Paradise Lot doctors told me.

I mean, here I was in Montreal, watching my normally helpless boyfriend take down birds with a bow and arrows. A bow and arrows! And not just taking them down. He was making shots I couldn't have made (and I grew up in an era when bow hunting was a thing).

He was as graceful as Aldie, and his hunting prowess would have made Egya—a born hunter—green with envy.

Justin was seriously badass.

I'd have been more impressed if I wasn't fixated on the other person with him: a young woman with curly red hair and pale skin. I guess you could say she was cute, if you were into that sort of thing.

OK Kat, get a hold of yourself. Your boyfriend—

I looked over at Justin as he took down another bird with a shot that would have made Robin Hood give him a high-five.

But as good as he is, those are a lot of birds. He needs help, I thought.

Another shot, then a third.

OK, maybe not. When did Justin get all Terminator-meets-Predator-like?

I shook my head. I could mull over such thoughts when I got to him. Right now, some birds needed felling. (Is that the term for taking down a flock of killer birds of prey?) Not sure … I'd figure out appropriate vocab later. Now he needed me.

Well, he needed monster-killing Kat.

And if I was going to be of use, I needed a weapon. Something that would be useful against these diving monsters.

But just as I was about to enter the fray, it ended. The birds started falling from the sky, and not just because of Justin's arrows. Something had happened, and the fracas came to a screeching, feathery halt.

Seems he didn't need monster killing Kat, after all.

I watched as the redhead ran to Justin and decided that the post-battle wrap-up perhaps wasn't the best time for me to re-enter his life. Besides, there was that girl, and—

Argh! Kat, stop acting like a thirteen-year-old, jealous biddy.

I shook my head and made my way to his frat house. I'd wait for him there and we'd figure out whatever we needed figuring out.

Biddy. Humph, now that's a word I knew no one used anymore.

↔

Waiting on the stoop of O³'s frat house was less fun than you'd think. First off, you're on a stoop, in February, in Montreal. It was damn cold ... and I wasn't just talking about the weather.

Justin's fellow fraters were more fidgety than any ice storm, giving me the stink eye as they walked in. I knew most of these guys. The GoneGods know I'd spend enough nights sleeping in this very house with them partying in the halls.

We had always engaged in friendly banter, a wee bit of harmless flirting and tons of trash talking when I took them down at ping pong.

But instead of the usual, "Hey girl!" and, "What's ups," the guys ignored me. All of them except the apu, Seth.

A while back Seth and I ... well, let's just say we took care of a murderous problem that was threatening the campus. Seth was an Aztec cave apu, a guardian spirit whose sole purpose for existence was to protect those who lived in his territory. He and I had formed a kinship when protecting the campus together.

Two kindred spirits doing what we needed to do.

So when Seth showed up, I expected a smile. Instead, he looked at me with his sky-blue eyes that slowly grew gray with worry and said, "You shouldn't have returned."

"Well, hello to you, too."

Seth shook his head and repeated, "You shouldn't have returned. Not here. Not now. Not ever."

Now that was a bit cheeky of him. I mean, Justin and I had fights, and yeah, we broke up after I failed to protect him from a dybbuk demon that possessed him for a couple weeks—but still. Seth's reaction to seeing me hurt.

"Look, what's between Justin and me is none of your—"

The apu shook his brown, rock-like head. "No, you misunderstand. This place—it is possessed. It is ..."—he paused as he searched for the word—"evolving into something that is cruel and unkind. But we have found an uneasy balance. Your presence will destroy that balance. Destroy the peace."

So that was it. He couldn't care less about the issues between Justin and me. He was worried about something else entirely.

I grabbed Seth's hand. It was coarse, like a thin filament of sand on leather, and being this close to him, I could smell the earth. And I don't mean the ground that I stood on. That was covered in snow, its scent hidden from noses as powerful as Egya's. What I mean is, from Seth I could smell the earth as if it was a cool spring day in some lush forest.

An apu's natural scent.

"Seth—I thought we were friends. What's going on—?"

"Attraction." He said that word like it explained everything.

It didn't.

"Attraction?" I tried to color my voice with all shades of confusion. Most of the time Others didn't clue into those verbal cues.

But Seth was a bit more adept at human nuances than most Others.

Seth smiled, revealing teeth the color of pearls. "Yes. Attraction." He chuckled, his expression softer, like he was remembering that we were friends. "As in, you are one who attracts."

"Hey, I know I'm cute, but—"

He waved a dismissive hand. "You hide behind your humor. But hiding now will only get you and those you love killed."

"OK," I said, shaking away the joke I had. Too bad—it was a doozy. "I think I understand. You think that my presence is somehow going to bring out the big nasties from the woodworks."

"No. Those monsters are already here. I think you are going to bring them to us." He leaned in close, pulling me toward him, and whispered in my ear, "They are changing. And with that change, they will bring destruction to the world. And your presence can only mean bad luck."

I pulled away to look at him. I mean, really look at him. His eyes were a stormy gray now, any hint of blue gone.

For most humans, bad luck wasn't real. Sure, crossing paths with black cats or walking under ladders often elicits the thought of *Did I just give myself some bad luck?* But that was a thought that most would quickly dismiss and forget.

Others are a suspicious bunch—but then again, wouldn't you be if you actually knew that magic, curses and hexes were real? And if that kind of stuff was real, then it stands to reason that bad luck is real, too.

But to Others, it was more than just a real concept. Accidently imbuing themselves with bad luck usually meant purification rituals and hiding until the timeframe of that bad luck passed.

So if he was going full superstitious Other on me, then the only thing I could do was go full Other on him. "Apu, cave entity and protector of the O^3 clan," I said, "if bad luck comes this way, tell me so I can do whatever is necessary to alter its course."

The apu shook his head. "The course is set. But you, Katrina, act like a pull, drawing it closer than it would otherwise come. You must leave."

He was serious. He really wanted me to go. As in, away. Leave this frat house, leave the campus, leave Montreal. "I cannot do that."

Seth nodded, pursing his lips with a solemn resolve. "Then prepare to lose much."

"Seth, please—tell me what's going on. Please."

"I can't, Kat. I was made to take an oath."

"By who?"

"Who do you think?" he said, gesturing behind him.

Shit, Others and their oaths. They took those kinds of things very seriously, and little could make them break it. Torture, threatening loved ones, even death would not move an Other to break an oath.

But the flip side to that was Others did not make an oath unless they didn't believe it absolutely necessary. This apu—this protector— took his oath because he believed keeping whatever secret he held would do more good than harm.

"OK," I said. "I will not ask you again. But I cannot go. Not until I know for sure that my presence is truly bad luck that will bring ruin here. Once I know that for sure, I will either do what I must to help, or I will leave."

"By then it will be too late."

"Perhaps," I said. "Bad luck and fate rarely end in carnivals and parties."

Seth smirked. "Indeed. The gods were sadistic when creating such concepts. Very well, but know that should things progress, I will do whatever I must to protect my brothers."

A threat? Absolutely. He had chosen this frat house and its members as his to protect. That meant he would go to the farthest extremes to shield them from danger.

Even if it meant killing someone he considered a friend.

"I understand."

"Good." He nodded behind me. "It seems you have attracted some of that bad luck already. He will be home soon. I can sense him."

And with that, the apu went inside to leave me alone, waiting for Justin. Given that he just told me I had attracted more bad luck, I could only assume that when Justin did turn up, he wouldn't be alone.

I waited for about an hour, alone and cold, until I saw Justin. He was holding the hand of the beautiful redhead, and she too looked surprised.

As soon as they saw me, his mouth opened wide in shock and surprise.

So did hers, only her surprise carried with it a hint of sadness, too.

"Hi Justin," I said, my eyes fixated on their clasped hands. "I see you've been busy."

2

CHEATING BOYFRIENDS AND BAD BREAKUPS

*J*ustin's hand let go of the other girl's, and I expected the typical groveling that you see in the movies. You know, the, *"Kat—it's not what you think"* or, *"She means nothing."*

But the trouble with movies is that script writers don't seem to live real lives, because things rarely go down the way they say they do.

Instead of guilt, instead of begging, he just locked eyes with me and said, "Where have you been?"

If he said it with a Scottish accent, circa 1808, he would have been my father.

"Excuse me?"

"You heard me. Where the hell have you been?"

"Funny you should use that word ..."

"No jokes, Kat. I've been worried sick about you."

"I can see that." I looked over at the girl by his side, who stared at me with eyes that held a mix of guilt and shame ... and admiration. I shook that last thought off. There wasn't any admiration there—she was a boyfriend-stealing skank, plain and simple.

Then again, Justin might not have told her about me ...

If Justin remembered that there was another woman by his side, he made no indication of it. His gaze was firmly locked on me. And in his eyes I saw something that I'd never seen before.

Fury.

But not the kind of petulant fury that young men have when the world doesn't treat them the way they think it should. This was an aged fury that was reserved for those who had experienced terrible things and knew that the world was wholly indifferent to their needs.

He looked older.

More cynical.

Like these last few weeks had aged him well beyond his nineteen years.

Not that any of that mattered now. Now we were having a lover's spat that would most likely end in our breakup, so I was in full, get-in-my-jabs-while-the-getting's-good mode. "And I see you know how to use a bow. When did that happen?"

"A lot has happened since you left."

"I've only been gone for a few weeks, Justin. You were shooting that thing like you were born with it."

He unslung his bow and casually walked to the front porch, placing it down there with an unnerving confidence. "I've been training."

"I've trained a lot in my life. Trust me, you don't get that good that quick. You can't."

Justin's hands were on the railing of the porch. He was squeezing the old wood like he was channeling his rage into it. It was as if he knew that letting go of the banister would result in him lashing out at me, maybe even trying to hurt me.

This wasn't the Justin I knew.

As angry as Justin could get, I never sensed any violence in him. He was the blue-eyed, happy-go-lucky kid who just wanted to help out and do good.

This Justin was something else.

"Something different," I muttered, and looking at the girl who hadn't moved, said, "I suspect you have something to do with it?"

She lifted an awkward hand in a weird kind of wave. "Hi, I'm Isabella. Isa to my friends."

"So, Isabella," I snipped. "I'd say it's nice to meet you, but …"

She seemed sad I didn't call her Isa. "Nice to meet you, too," she said, forcing a smile.

"So you're an Other."

"How … How did you know?" She was touching her face, feeling around for some telltale sign that might have given her away.

"The wave. Your ridiculous reaction to seeing me. You clearly know who I am, but you don't act like you do. You don't act like any normal human would in this situation."

Isabella nodded. "I know. I've just been in situations like this so often. I mean, not that often. But enough times to know that if I beg for your forgiveness, it'll only infuriate you more. And if I run, you'll feel justified in your hatred. But if I stand here and treat this situation for what it is, then eventually you'll let go."

"And what is this situation, exactly?"

"Justin must choose," she said in a flat tone. She wanted him to choose her. That was obvious. But she'd also accept if he didn't.

I shook my head. "No, I'm not something that he gets to decide on. No one chooses me. I choose *them*." There was an old hate in me when I said that. Something I hadn't really felt since my vampire days.

When I was the hunter, I chose my victims with a kind of detached malevolence. Like it was my privilege to kill them. That sense of privilege was pouring out of me with all its shades of ugly.

Justin snorted. "That's the problem, isn't it? You chose them. And you chose me. Then you un-chose me. And now you're back because … what? You want me again? You're playing with me like I'm some kind of toy or something."

He still held onto the banister, his back to me, and I could sense the pain he was feeling. That hit me like a wave of heat, and I realized the old demon in me was rearing its ugly head.

That wasn't me. Not anymore … right?

I let out a long sigh as my voice softened. "I didn't mean it like that."

15

"No, you didn't mean to say it out loud like that. Maybe it was one of your quirky, out-loud thoughts, or just that you wanted to hurt Isa and me ... but wherever it came from, you're telling the truth. You really do think you get to choose."

With those last words, I knew I had lost. Lost him. Lost the right to be hurt and angry about all this. I was the bad guy in this little exchange. The one who left him after the dybbuk demon possessed him. The one who went away without a word and stayed gone for weeks. And now I was the one who expected all to be forgiven just because I wanted it to be so.

"I'm sorry." I lifted my head up to stop a tear from escaping. "You're right. I'm being an asshole. I should—"

"No," he growled, letting go of the banister as he turned to face me. As soon as his hands were off the wooden rail, I saw indents in the shape of his fingers. He had held onto the railing so hard he'd squeezed the wood, molding it under his grip. Sure the wood was old, but still ... when the hell did he get so strong?

"No," he repeated. "You don't even get to be the apologetic bitch who owns her mistakes so you feel better about yourself. All you get to do is leave. Leave, leave. Leave!"

The last word came out with such hatred that I swear the Gone-Gods must have heard. "OK," I said, my voice low. "I'll go. For what it's worth, I'm—"

But before I could finish my words, he stomped up the steps and went inside.

The girl, Isabella, didn't move.

"What? Not going in?" I said. "I think we know who he chose."

The beautiful Other shook her head. "He hasn't chosen. All he has decided right now is that he does not want to choose you. But the passion he has for you—the anger—can only come from true love. He loves you still," she said, "and until that is tempered, he will always choose you, even when bedding me."

I narrowed my eyes in confusion. *What brutal honesty. What an ability to see things as they are and not as you want them to be. What kind of Other is she?*

Isabella looked at me. "Thank you," she said. Damn it. Out loud again. "I am an encantado from the Amazon. And although you may not believe this, the only reason Justin even caught my attention was because of you."

"What the hell does that mean?"

"You are so confident even though you lost just as much as I did."

"So you know what I was before the gods left," I said. "Justin tell you?"

"I know because, much like what you said about me, you, too, have your awkward, non-human ways."

"Humph," I said, a wee bit hurt. I always prided myself on being an excellent poker player, hiding my hand. Seems I wasn't as good at that as I thought.

"And despite having lost your immortality, you are so ..."—she searched for the word—"complete."

"I don't know about that." Staring at her, I saw not only beauty, but an unbridled intelligence. Like she *thought* on another level. No, that's not right. It was as if she could think on multiple levels at once. I could see what Justin liked about her.

Hell, I was starting to like her.

"And part of that completeness comes because of him." She nodded at the frat house.

"Well, that's over now."

She shook her head. "No, that is far from over."

It was a bit weird getting a pep talk from Isabella, given that she clearly had feelings for Justin and wanted me out of the picture. "Ahh, you have a good shot, too," I said.

What the hell was I doing encouraging her?

She smiled. "Thank you. I do. But not today. Today he needs to be alone to contemplate his desires."

"Whatever," I said, coming to my sense. "Like I said, I out. I'm not someone to be chosen, and even if I did want him back and he wanted me ... we're no good together. I'm no good for him. I only bring him pain."

"Perhaps."

What? No more encouraging words? And after I gave her a wee pep talk ...

I shook my head. "OK, as much as I'm enjoying this little ... whatever this is ... I think I should leave." I took two steps before the little nag in the back of my head took over. "Isa ... I mean, Isabella. How did he get so good with a bow? And strong, too?"

"He's joined the World Army Cadet program," she said, her face painted with the same concern I was feeling. "Their training is intensive. They use cutting-edge technology—VR, and other stuff—to enhance their abilities."

"I've heard about VR training, but it can't give them *that*," I said, looking at the banister.

She looked at the warped wood and nodded. "No ... no, it can't."

3

GUILTY FEET HAVE GOT NO
RHYTHM

"I can't believe he's already with someone else," I said. "Sure, it's been close to five weeks since I last saw Justin, but let me debunk a myth for you all—time does not heal all wounds."

"Five weeks isn't time," Egya snickered. "Not when you're three hundred years old. You operate on another timescale."

"So how long until this icky feeling goes away?"

Egya shrugged. "A decade?"

"I don't have a decade."

"Do you wish me to rip off his treacherous arms and beat this new lover with them?" Deirdre said.

"Yes."

Deirdre stood up.

"No, no ... I was joking."

Deirdre looked me up and down with suspicious eyes. "Were you? You wear no smile, and your body is tense like one who waits for battle."

"You know, you have a very simplistic way of seeing things, my changeling friend."

"Thank you."

"It wasn't a compliment."

"Are you sure?" She tilted her head in confusion. "Another mirthless joke, perhaps?"

"Yeah, another mirthless joke."

There was cackle from the corner of our room. Egya was sitting on Deirdre's bed, practicing elongating and retracting his fingertips into claws. "You did break up with him, didn't you?"

"Yeah, I know … but it wasn't a *breakup* breakup. It was a 'We need a break' breakup."

"This is feeling like a rerun of one of the worst subplots in *Friends* all over again."

"Friends?" Deirdre said. "We are all friends here, are we not?"

"It's a TV show."

"Friends on TV. Friends in real life." She touched my shoulder.

Deciding not to explain the whole Ross and Rachael debacle, I just nodded. "Friends forever."

Deirdre crossed her hands over her chest and bowed in a solemn, very serious manner. "Friends forever."

"OK, enough of this," I said. "I just broke up with my boyfriend. And human-made movies all say the same thing when a beautiful girl like me needs to mend her heart … time to go dancing."

Egya smirked. "I thought it was Häagen-Dazs."

"No, silly," I chuckled. "That was last week. This week it's about going out, getting drunk, potentially making a bad decision with the wrong guy who's just going to use me."

Deirdre pursed her lips, pounding her fist into her open palm. "Who is this wrong person who will use you? I swear that I—"

"Deirdre, honey. I'm talking about a one-night stand of meaningless whoopie."

"Why do you always use that word when talking about sex?" Egya said.

"Making whoopie. Ella Fitzgerald used it in one of her songs."

"I know the reference. I just don't understand why you constantly use it?"

I smirked. "If you had ever seen her in concert, you'd know. I swear to the GoneGods, one of my greatest regrets was not turning Ella into a vampire. She was divine."

"It wouldn't be the same," Egya chuckled. "Blood ruins the vocal cords."

"Whatever," I said, grabbing Eyga's hand and pulling him off the bed. "You get out of here while we girls get ready." I sniffed him. "Go take a shower and put on some cologne. You smell like wet dog."

"Yes ma'am," he said, saluting me.

"And be ready to leave here at twenty-hundred hours."

"Yes ma'am. Right away, ma'am," he said, leaving the room.

I turned to my changeling roommate. "Now you—let's get you dolled up, honey."

"Dolled up? What is dolled up?"

"Oh, you'll see."

↔

Egya knocked on our door at exactly eight o'clock, dressed like he was out of *Saturday Night Fever*. He wore an almost glowing white suit that contrasted with his black shirt like the keys on a piano. His black shoes were so shiny that they were practically dark mirrors, and he wore a thick gold chain around his neck.

"Seriously?" I said.

Normally I'd expect Egya to say something ridiculous about the times, or how Travolta was really a were-hyena or something ridiculous like that. But instead, the Ghanaian's eyes widened when he saw me, and he did something I didn't think Egya was capable of.

He stuttered.

"Ahh, you ... look ... I mean ..." He finally stopped his chattering and took a deep breath. "You look amazing."

"You mean this old thing." I had meant it as a joke, but the truth was, I was wearing the same dress that Audrey Hepburn wore in

Breakfast at Tiffany's. It was old, something I had purchased from the original designer. And even though I was slightly chestier than the actress, it fit me perfectly. As well it should; Givenchy altered it just for me—as in, personally—and I looked so beautiful in it that I rewarded him by *not* eating him afterward.

"No, seriously. You look amazing," he repeated.

I was pulling out all the stops tonight. I was dressed to kill, applying centuries of knowledge on the art of seduction. Tonight was my getting-over-the-boy night, and you could only do that when you looked amazing. Still ...

I narrowed my eyes. This wasn't the kind of reaction I'd expected from Egya. Mortal human boys who weren't my friend, sure. But Egya? "Are you feeling OK?"

"Ahhh, I'll be right back," he said, and ran off.

"What?" I yelled after him. "Where are you going?"

"I'll be ten minutes. Just wait." And with that, he was gone.

"Milady," Deirdre said, peering out in the hall in her typical centurion ways, like she was looking for an intruder or something.

"What is it, Deirdre?"

"I fear that our dorm has been infiltrated by ..."—she turned, giving me the biggest, most hammed-up smile ever—"Cupid."

Then she just stood there, waiting for my reaction.

"Are you making a joke?"

Her smile widened. "You recognized my humor. I was successful."

"Yeah ... yeah you were," I said, staring down the hall after a boy with whom my relationship had just gotten a wee bit more complicated.

↔

"Egya and I are friends," I said.

My words were coming out jumbled and slurred, like slushy ice pouring out of a machine.

The girl in the bathroom nodded. "That's because you're drunk," she said, and from her slushy machine-style slurring, I could tell she was drunk, too.

"You're right," I said. "I'm getting over a boy. Hence this dress."

"You look gorgeous, by the way," said the stranger whom I'd just met in the toilet of the club. And even though we'd just met, I knew we'd be friends forever.

If I remembered any of this tomorrow, that was.

"Audrey Hepburn in *Breakfast at Tiffany's*."

"Who?"

"Audrey Hepburn."

"Like I said, who?"

"You know, Miss …" then I realized I was talking to some nineteen-year-old mortal who'd probably never even heard of Audrey Hepburn, let alone any movie she had starred in. "Never mind."

"Whatever. So you and Iggy are just friends?"

"Eg-ya," I said. "And yes, friends. But tonight he's acting all weird. You know, in that way that guys get when they're interested in making whoopie."

"Making what?"

"Whoopie."

The drunk girl gave me a blank look.

I sighed. "Ella Fitzgerald?"

"Ella who?"

"Never mind." Remember her tomorrow or not, we weren't destined to be friends, as I could never break bread with someone who didn't know Ella. "The point is, we're just friends. And now that I'm single, he's all 'opening doors' and being polite. No more stupid jokes. No more irritating snickering."

"And that's a bad thing?" She turned to the mirror to reapply her lipstick.

"Yeah. I like the snickering."

"You just said it was irritating."

23

"I know, but it's what makes him *him*."

She turned, pointing the lipstick at me like a lecture stick. "Are you talking about that tall, dark and handsome man you were dancing with out there? The guy with the dark-gray blazer?"

"Yeah."

"He's hot. Great dresser, too."

"Yeah," I repeated. And it was true. When Egya returned to our dorm twenty minutes after running off, he wasn't wearing that ridiculous 70s suit anymore, having traded it for something a lot more elegant and modern. A beautiful wool blazer and pristine khakis, black shoes with a hint of red in them and no more gold chain.

He looked amazing. As in, stutteringly so.

"What's the problem?" the not-going-to-be-my-friend-tomorrow girl asked. "Super-hot guy. Looks like he'd be a tornado in bed, too. Go for it."

"But we're friends. And my boyfriend ..."

"*Ex*."

"Ex-boyfriend. We just broke up, and besides ... Egya is my ..."

"Friend," she echoed. "You know what friends are? The lovers you wish you had if you'd just get out of your own head."

Inexpertly wise. "And what if it ruins our friendship?"

"Better that than die wondering." She pursed her lips against a sheet of toilet paper. "How do I look?"

"Like Brigitte Bardot."

"Are you foreign or something? You keep referring to people I don't know."

"I guess so," I said. "But not from another country. Just another era." Did I really just say that out loud?

She narrowed her eyes before popping her lipstick back into her purse and heading for the door. "You're weird," she said, turning to look at me from the exit. "If super-hot guy likes you despite that, then go for it, because most guys would go running."

I shrugged. "I think he actually likes my kind of weird."

"Marry him, girl. Marry him."

24

↔

I stepped out of the bathroom and back into the thumping bass of 50 Cent's "It's Your Birthday." Walking over to our table, I saw Deirdre on the dance floor, flailing her arms and legs about like a toddler being instructed to do so by a clown at … well, a birthday.

Fae dancing.

It's less about rhythm and more about movement. The more of it, the better.

The dance floor was filled mostly with humans—who gave Deirdre a wide berth—and a few Others who did their own version of dancing. Two pixies were Irish stepdancing completely out of sync with 50 Cent's song, a gnome hopped up and down in place and a leshy stood perfectly still—the tree creature's version of tearing up the dance floor, I guess.

There was also the biggest centaur I'd ever seen stepping back in forth in place like he was doing a horse's version of the Running Man. Seriously—the half-man, half-horse was huge.

And who wasn't on the dance floor? Egya. He was at our table with a fresh drink in hand. "Another vodka and soda?" I asked, knowing the ploy. Get me super drunk and, wham, bam, making-whoopie slam.

Arrgh, even I get annoyed at my kind of weird.

"Actually, it's water," he said. "You've had quite a bit tonight."

So he wasn't trying to get me drunk; he was being a nice guy. The jerk was making this harder for me.

"Egya," I started, taking a deep breath. Best to get this out in the open now. "What are you—?"

"When the gods left, the hardest thing for me was losing my sense of smell."

"Excuse me?"

"My sense of smell. That I couldn't become a hyena anymore was one thing, but I also lost certain abilities I'd had when I was in my human form. Smell, hearing, taste. It was smell that struck me the hardest. Things were just dull when your nose was no longer a thousand times more sensitive than that of a human's. It was kind of like suddenly becoming blind."

"I get it," I said. "I lost my senses, too. My sense of smell also dulled. I doubt I had your kind of nose, but I could always rely on it to forewarn me of what was coming. As a vampire, I'd take a deep breath before entering a room and the smells that greeted me told me exactly who or what was on the other side of that door before I opened it."

"And food. Human noses don't tell you anything about what you're about to eat."

"Yeah, no kidding. As a human, all blood smells like this coppery, metallic substance. But as a vampire, everyone's blood smelled different. I knew how old you were, where you were from, your blood type, if you had any diseases just by one sniff."

"And what about butts …"

"What?"

He snickered. "Because hyenas are like dogs. Dogs sniff butts …"

Here was the old Egya I knew. I laughed. "Vamps weren't into butts."

"Everyone's into butts." He took a deep breath. "When the gods left and I lost my sense of smell, I felt like a part of me had been ripped away. I fell into a deep depression."

"But you're always so chipper."

"Chipper? I'm from Ghana, and even *I* know people in Canada don't use the word 'chipper' anymore."

"Hey, it's making a comeback."

"Sure it is … Anyway, I wasn't chipper. I was just trying to find a way to be human again. I was doing everything I could just to survive. After a couple years, I got used to things, but that cloud of loss never fully left me." He took another deep breath. "But now my sense of smell is back."

"How?"

"I'm never fully human anymore," he said. "Some things don't completely leave me no matter what form I'm in. I can smell and see just like I used to. Well, not quite as well I used to," he corrected, "but damn close. The cloud no longer follows me, and without it dampening my soul, I can see—*smell*—a path that I did not believe was for me. I'm finally free." He took a step closer to me, grabbing my hand as he did.

"Free to do what?" I asked, my breath quickening.

He took one final deep breath like he was psyching himself up to kiss me. And I honestly didn't know how I'd react. He leaned in close, but before our lips met, his eyes darted behind me. "Duck."

"What?"

In answer, he fell backward, pulling me to the ground with him.

4
PISSING CONTESTS AREN'T JUST FOR BOYS

A beer bottle came flying past me and smashed on the wall near where we stood. *Oh great*, I thought, *a bar fight*. But instead of hearing the usual posturing of boys playing the tough guys, I heard snorts and braying as heavy feet stomped on the linoleum flooring.

Another inner-species fight? Humans picking on some Others or some shit like that. The problem with most of these fights was that Others never fought back, and for good reason. No matter the circumstances, they tended to be the ones that went to jail.

And once in jail, there were enough horror stories about them not understanding human laws and getting terribly long jail terms for simply defending themselves.

It was common practice for an Other to simply take their lumps and leave. Better than getting a three-year sentence for pushing a stupid, testosterone-filled kid back.

That was just one of the injustices of the GoneGod World—but at least it was an injustice I could do something about. I was human. At least, I was now. I could get involved. I could smash some aggro boy in the face, and when the cops came, they'd take one look at my five-

28

foot-nothing, dainty frame and not believe them when they pointed their blood-covered hands at me.

Besides, they weren't the only ones filled with alcohol-fueled rage.

Oh, hell no. Here I come to save the day.

"Girl, you're drunk," Egya said.

Shit, did I think that out loud? Never mind. I gave Egya one of my it's-about-to-get-real smiles and turned, expecting to see the gaggle of boys pushing some poor Other.

But instead, I saw the massive centaur grabbing two of the pixies as he menacingly advanced on the poor, quivering gnome. Up close, I noticed that he wore a blue, pin-striped shirt from Abercrombie and Fitch. He had style. In fact, he had my boyfriend's style. He wore a similar Abercrombie and Fitch shirt to the one I had bought Justin for his birthday.

Oh great, I'm so not over him that I'm noticing his shirt in a fight. I could just hear Egya's voice in my head saying, *"Girl—you need to get your head straight."*

Both the leshy and Deirdre were standing up for the gnome, hands out as they shielded the gnome from the centaur.

A minotaur got up from the bar and muttered something in ancient Greek. Even though I couldn't understand what the bull-headed creature was saying, I knew from his gestures he was pleading with the centaur to calm down.

The minotaur was massive—they all are—and generally speaking, a minotaur and centaur would be evenly matched in both size and strength. But this centaur was something else, towering over the minotaur by three feet.

I ran into the fray and put up my arms. "Dude. What are you doing? You're attacking an Other. Why?"

"The foolish creature stood under me."

"So?"

"Centaurs do not like anything standing under them. It is an insult to their kind," the minotaur said in a very heavy Greek accent.

"I didn't stand under you," the gnome said. "I was jumping up and down in place. You stood *over* me!"

"That's true, that's true," cried out one of the pixies. "Everyone knows gnomes can't dance. They just hop. In place. Like a bouncing ball."

"A boring bouncing ball," said the other pixie.

"My brother," the minotaur said, "it was a simple misunderstanding. Please, let us not bring more trouble on ourselves. This GoneGod World is already full—"

Before the minotaur could finish his last words, the centaur threw one of the pixies into his chest, which bounced off like, well ... a bouncing ball. Then he threw the second pixie at the leshy and charged.

Oh goodie, I get to fight a horse.

↔

How do you fight a centaur? The same way you fight any boy when the goal is to get him down as quickly as possible: kick him in the balls. Not an easy feat when dealing with a huge, powerful creature.

Still, he had a huge undercarriage that housed huge ... well ... boy parts. I waited for him to rear up, and rolled under him. As I did, I noted that both Deirdre and the leshy were trying to grab his arm as Egya jumped on his back. We were going for the old overpower-and-encumber move. Awesome. Now all I needed to do was strike with one well-placed fist and he should go down.

Once the centaur was on his side, we could hold him until he either calmed down or the authorities showed up with horse-sized handcuffs (you'd be surprised what the police carry on them these days).

But when I was under, I didn't see the expected white fur typical of the underbelly of a horse. Instead, there were green, half-moon shells all over him. They looked like fish scales or ... "Dragon scales," I muttered. This guy was wearing the Other equivalent of a jock strap.

I should have rolled away as soon as I realized my plan wouldn't work. But I was too drunk and slow. A heavy, hooved foot cracked the floor inches away from my pretty head.

Shit, I wasn't noticing the kinds of things I should have been when fighting a creature like this. Things like the fact that both Deirdre and the leshy weren't really able to hold him down. Things like the fact that Egya was parallel to me, also lying on the floor, which meant he'd been thrown off.

I was alone, and all this guy needed to do was keep stomping until he caught a piece of moi.

I tried to roll away, but every move I made was met with a denying hoof that forced me back under. It was only a matter of time. I needed rescuing, and it was only appropriate that the club started playing the dance version of "Waiting for a Hero" when someone tackled the centaur with such force that he fell over onto his side. This guy was fast.

The centaur tried to get back up, but my savior landed one well-aimed fist on the horse man's face and he was out. Not only was this guy fast, he was strong, too.

I got up, expecting my savior to be some kind of super-powered Other. You know, the Superman equivalent of an elf or a drow.

But when he turned, instead of being greeted by pointy ears or the over-sized black eyes, I was met with a chiseled jaw that would have made Captain America green with envy and the lush black hair of an Adonis.

"Hey Kat. Surprised?"

"Ahh, Justin?"

↔

"Ahh, Justin, how did you get so … you know … so?" I fumbled to find the words.

"Like I said, I've been training."

Justin offered me a hand, helping me to my feet. As he did, three other boys—*human* boys—went for the centaur, making sure he was down. They cuffed the creature with huge ankle bracelets, and one of them put a leash around the still-downed centaur's head.

All of them, including Justin, wore the same army-green shirts and cargo pants with an emblem of three circles interlaced. The only difference was that with the World Army's logo, there was a dove carrying an olive branch.

Memnock Securities did not pretend to hold such values.

Still, they shared the same basic logo, and I found it odd that the two organizations—one private, one not—had the such similar emblems.

"What's going on?"

"I'm part of, um, campus security. We patrol the area and deal with upstarts like this guy."

The centaur was coming round. I braced myself for another fight —some kicking, something. But as soon as the centaur realized what was happening—and who was doing it to him—he just stood up and, hanging his head low, let the boy-soldiers lead him out.

The centaur knew these guys. Had faced them before. And unlike when getting into a fight with a super-powerful leshy, changeling, minotaur, two pixies and a couple humans, he knew he was outmatched.

What the hell was going on?

Justin must have sensed the wheels turning in my head, because he shot me one of those smiles he used when he did something impressive and knew it (usually the smile he gave post ... ahhh, whoopie, the cheeky bastard). "We got a rep going. Training is intense, but we're making a difference. Anyway, I got to get this guy to processing, so ..."

"So ... you got to go," I said with a wee bit too much yearning in my voice.

Justin started to walk away, but stopped and came back over to me. "You know, things ended badly, and I'm sorry. I said things I shouldn't have. Getting over you was the hardest thing I've ever had to do."

"And you just took down the biggest centaur I've ever seen, so doing hard things is kind of your thing."

He chuckled. It was good to hear him laugh. "Yeah, maybe. But I just want you to know, I'm not angry. Not anymore. Going through all the shit I went through with you showed me my purpose. I know who I want to be now."

"A soldier?"

"A man who will make a difference. Other and humans—we'll eventually figure out a way to live together. But not any time soon. We're going to fumble our way through this, and while we do there will be lots of these kinds of encounters. The world needs people like us"—he gestured at the two of us—"to help smooth things over. So thank you, Kat. Really, thank you."

"Thank you?"

"Breaking my heart made me stronger." He stuck out a hand in a good, sportsmanlike fashion—like we'd just finished a rigorous game of tennis or something.

I looked at it with genuine confusion. "And you want to shake hands?"

"Humph, yeah. Not quite what I meant, but I wasn't sure what else to do." He tucked away his hand before he eyes lit up with an idea. "Tell you what? Why don't we have a drink."

"I don't know—"

"Not like that," he said. "O³—we're having a party tomorrow. It's a small thing, really. Just a few friends. Why don't you, Deirdre and Egya come along?" He nodded at my two friends who were hovering just far enough to give us our privacy, but not too far that they couldn't hear what we were saying. "During that party, I'll come up to you like we're old friends who haven't seen each other in a while and we'll catch up. Casual-like and friendly."

Damn, Justin wasn't only faster and stronger—he was smoother, too.

"Ahh, OK," I said in my own smooth-like-silk way. Of course, drunk and befuddled, I doubted I sounded anything other than what I was … a smitten, lovelorn, confused ex-girlfriend.

"Good. See you tomorrow." And before I could say anything else, he walked away.

As soon as she was gone, Deirdre rushed to my side. "Milady," she said, her voice full of unbridled excitement. "Before, when you bedded the human—I was confused. He was weak and wilting. But now he is not. When did Justin get so powerful and attractive?"

"Yeah, when indeed," I muttered.

5

HANGOVERS AND HANG-UPS

*M*y head throbbed like the drummer to Metallica had taken up residence in there. I swear to the GoneGods I wished for death.

Death or Tylenol—whichever was easier. I groaned as I turned over in my bed. There on the floor, covered with a quilt made of leaves, lay Deirdre. The poor changeling must have also been hungover, because she rubbed two rotting banana peels on her temples.

Fae home remedies.

"Milady," she groaned, "why does my head hurt so?"

"It's called a hangover, Deirdre," I said, the effort of speaking almost unbearable. "You just need water."

"I need a new head."

"You and me too," I said, trying to get up as my hand fumbled through my purse for a painkiller.

I found some ibuprofen. "Take two of these." Then, remembering a changeling's constitution, added, "Better make it three and call me in the morning."

"It is the morning."

"It was … You know what, you're right." I popped two pills, swallowed them dry and rolled over.

"I do not understand this pain. Before the gods left, I could will away such discomfort. But now … perhaps I should burn some time to make this go away."

"No," I said, the effort causing the Metallica drummer to rage into a drum solo. "No … don't. This is part of being mortal. You have to get used to it."

"You do indeed," said a cackling voice. "But it does get better, I promise."

Egya entered carrying with him the only true remedy for a hangover—greasy food and coffee.

I sat up, ripping the double bacon and sausage roll out of its paper bag with greedy hands and biting in like it was my last meal. "Oh wow," I said, chewing, "I think I love you."

Egya's eyes darted away and he sat down on the ground next to Deirdre, handing her a heaping dish of poutine. The fae Other looked at the plate of French fries, gravy and melted curd cheese with utter confusion. "What monstrous hell is this?"

"The ultimate hangover cure," I muttered, leaning over and stealing a fry. "I'll eat it if you don't."

Deirdre held the dish out of my reach before taking a bite. Her face lit up. She took another. Then a third, and before you could say, "Changeling, warrior and fae," she was munching away and making cooing sounds that gave me real insight into her lovemaking soundtrack.

"I think we have a winner," Egya said.

"We do indeed."

We ate the rest of our meal in silence before I finally had the strength to speak. "Egya—how is it that you have so much energy? I can barely move."

"The healing power of the hyena," he said.

"You didn't drink that much."

He lifted two fingers.

"And me?"

"I don't have enough fingers, girl."

"Ahh, I see."

"Is there more?" Deirdre asked as she licked her plate.

Egya chuckled. "I figured a changeling's appetite would be great." And he pulled out another dish from the bag.

"Oh thank you, great spotted dog." Deirdre ripped open the take-away packaging's lid and dug in.

"You?" Egya asked me. "I have a sausage roll and another poutine."

"Thanks, but that was perfect." I crumpled up the paper bag and threw it at the bin. It hit the side and fell on the floor with an uncere-monious thud.

"Good," Egya said, munching away at his own greasy monstrosity. Whatever he might have been going through yesterday with all the weirdness seemed to have vanished with this impromptu breakfast.

I sipped at my coffee, letting the ibuprofen goodness mix with the caffeine. Slowly, I was becoming human again. Which was funny, because when I actually did become human again, it was instant and painless. If the gods saw fit to suddenly make us half-breeds human again, you'd think they'd extend the courtesy to hangovers, too.

"So girl, will you go tonight?"

"Huh?" I said, my muddled brain trying to connect his words. "Oh … you mean Justin's party? Not sure yet." I tried to sound casual, but the thought of it made me want to re-assume the fetal position.

He rolled his eyes. "Why do you always fight who you are, girl? First you deny your past, and now this."

Here goes Egya again. Always wanting me to embrace who I was, like doing so would complete me or something. And this was becoming our pattern. He'd bait me into talking about something I hated talking about, and we'd get into a fight like some old married couple, which would inevitably end with him cracking a joke and resetting the whole thing.

"You're really about me accepting my past. Only thing is, I think I have."

He tilted his head down and gave me a look that clearly said he didn't agree.

"What? I have." I pointed to where my Cherub mask was hidden. "You know, the whole masked crusader saving the word to make up for the evil I've done … yadda, yadda, yadda." I took another bite.

"That's not accepting your past. That's apologizing for it."

"And?"

"And, girl, that is not good, either. You will never find—"

"If you say, 'peace,' I swear to the GoneGods I think I'll puke."

Egya shook his head, his face solemn. "No, girl. One like you will never find peace. I was going to say, 'purpose.' "

"And what would that 'purpose' be?" A bit of grease dribbled down my hand and I licked it up … in a very lady-like fashion. "Let me guess. Wear the mask and yadda, yadda, yadda."

Deirdre narrowed her eyes in confusion. "What's this yadda, yadda, yadda you speak of?"

"I'll tell you later," I said, currently lacking the patience to explain conversation shortcuts to the changeling. "And you, Hyena Boy—what's my purpose?"

Egya shook his head. "Yes, your purpose would be to still adorn the mask."

"Ah-ha!"

"But"—he lifted a silencing hand—"right now your actions are apologies. Not purpose."

"And the difference being?"

"One is eating junk food for instant gratification. The other is akin to nourishing your soul."

Dang, Egya made a good point. But we were in old-married-couple mode, which meant I couldn't actually acknowledge as much. That's what marriage is all about, right? Tit for tat and keeping score?

So I bit down hard on my terrible-for-your-soul sandwich. "I don't know. This food is pretty good."

"If I had more eyes to roll, I would. But mark my words, girl … one day you will understand the difference. Until then"—he took a sip from his coffee—"we have a party to attend."

"Party?" I muttered, feigning like I'd forgotten. "Oh, that. I'm not going."

"Yes, you are going, and you are going to want us with you."

"I ... will ... be ... by ... your ... side," Deirdre said between munches. "Always."

"Thanks, Deirdre. And as for you, how can you be so sure I'll go?"

"Three reasons." He lifted a finger. "One, you just broke up with him and it is part of the post-breakup game to prove to one another that you are fine. Second"—he raised another one—"something is different about Justin. Unnatural. I know you suspect magic. As do I."

"And I," Deirdre chimed in.

"You're going to want to sniff around to prove your theory right. And lastly"—he lifted one more, final finger—"you're a cat, and we all know what's going to kill you in the end."

"Curiosity?" I sneered.

"No, girl. Your need to be right," he cackled, sending all kinds of fresh pain through my head. "You're going to find magic at play, and it will probably kill you."

"Fine," I said, thinking about what Seth warned me about. Bad luck and all. He'd basically begged me to stay away. I wouldn't, and that would probably get me killed ... just like Egya said. "You got me. I'm going, and so are you two."

He crossed his arms over his chest. "How can you be so sure we'll go?"

Now it was my turn to lift up fingers. But unlike Egya, I only lifted my middle one and held it up to him. "Deirdre will go because Deirdre will always go."

Deirdre pounded her chest and let out a burp. "I am nourished and ready, milady."

"See? And as for you ... you're a dog. And dogs are nothing if they aren't loyal."

"Bow-wow," he snickered.

↔

Getting ready for the party was harder than it seemed, because I needed to balance being the right level of hot while not coming off as trying too hard. So after about a dozen outfits, I eventually settled on Levi's with a pink Mango, V-neck blouse.

And to balance it all out, I put on the pin that my father had used to hold his kilt, well, closed—an old silver dagger about three inches long, encased in a ring shaped like a thistle. I pinned it on my sweater's neck so that its weight pulled down the fabric just enough to reveal another centimeter of my bosom.

Hey, all's fair in love and war. Cleavage drives guys crazy, and I wasn't about to *not* use one of my best assets (and I think I deserve points for *not* using the obvious pun here, ahem).

I'd need the strength of my ancestors to get through this night. Egya came down in jeans and a t-shirt, and Deirdre wore a simple green dress that she simplified by meticulously lacing in pine needles all over her. She looked like a porcupine and smelled like a car freshener. She also wore the biggest smile that fended off any comments Egya and I might have made.

You do you, changeling. You do you.

By the time we got to the frat house, the party was well underway. Good, I was late enough that Justin would be doubting if I'd show up at all. I had him exactly where I wanted him.

But as soon as I stepped inside, I saw him standing next to that girl, their hands interlaced. She was wearing a cute little number from Mango, and she was obviously employing the same cleavage attack I was. And I swear to the GoneGods, her boobs were bigger than when I last saw her.

Figures—shapeshifter. For sure she's inflating them. Game on, encantado. Come on!

Justin's back was turned, so he didn't notice me, but she did. And as soon as our eyes locked, she let go of Justin's hand, said something to him and walked away.

Justin turned around. Seeing us, he grabbed a tray of plastic cups and walked over. "Hey guys, want a drink?"

Egya grabbed a cup with his usual enthusiasm. "Thank you, man. You look good. Been working out?"

Justin smirked. "You could say that."

Deirdre, being fae and a stickler for protocol and loyalty, didn't move, waiting for me to signal my OK to take a drink, which I did by grabbing my own cup. As soon as I had a cup in my hand, she took one, too.

"So glad you guys could make it." Justin looked at me. "I've got a couple hosting duties I need to do, and then I'll come over to, you know, have our casual conversation." He gave me a wink, walking away before I could think of anything witty to say.

GoneGodDamn it, any upper hand I had just vanished with that wink.

↔

Justin's hosting duties took longer than expected, because I was standing around pretending to enjoy this party for an hour before anyone came up to me. At first I thought he was just making me wait. But then I'd see him walking through the party with a concerned look in his eyes. And when I saw him with a couple guys talking to a guy who was clearly freaking out, I knew that he actually had a real problem on his hands.

The freaking-out guy—who was larger than the other three combined—had a look of panic, and even though he was on the other side of the room, I noticed the whites of his eyes. Or rather, the *lack* of … They had more of a blue tinge to them, and my first thought was, *What are these kids up to these days?*

Two girls gave me a weird look before giggling and whispering to themselves as they walked away.

God, I'm old.

Sometimes I wished I looked my age. Then again, looking my age probably meant I'd be a dust bunny under the bed, as I'm pretty sure three hundred years was long enough for my body to fully decompose.

Eventually Justin and the others disappeared, probably to take the guy home. Which meant Justin would be back soon, right? I tried to dance away the night with Deirdre and Egya ... Well, with Egya at least—Deirdre was doing her wild arm-flailing dance again, and I need to give her space lest I risk a black eye.

After about an hour of that, Justin returned. Finally. I made my way to the drinks counter, lingering there as long as I could, waiting for him to come back for a refill while pretending to pour myself a glass of punch. Harder than it seems. Luckily, I was a three-hundred-year-old ex-vampire who was an expert at sleight of hand.

A gentle hand touched my shoulder. Finally. I turned, expecting to see Justin's smile, but instead I was greeted by the last face I wanted to see—Isabella.

"Ahh, hi," I said, unable to hide my confusion.

She looked around sheepishly before sighing before blurting out, "You inspire me." Her eyes were slightly bloodshot, and she had a thousand-yard stare to her.

"OK ..." I said, drawing out the word.

She covered her mouth with embarrassment before letting out a giggle. "I'm sorry, I didn't mean it that way. I'm very stoned."

"So I've gathered."

"You see, I'm a biologist and I've grown my own strain. It's a bit different. You get all the fun without the munchies. But it does have this weird side effect. It tends to make you more honest and talkative." She held out a hand with two fountain pen-sized blunts in them.

"But the world needs more honesty, doesn't it?" she said. "And Justin told me all about your thinking-out-loud thing. This kind of does the same thing. Only you have to be stoned for it to work—unlike with you, where it seems to happen all the time."

"Again ... ok." She was talking so fast that I was finding it hard to keep up. To borrow a phrase from the 1970s, we weren't on the same wavelength.

"But all that is to say, I do admire you. I told you that already. But what I didn't get to say was that I'm sorry for what I did. I should have never pretended to be you. You were gone for so long, and he was so sad, so I thought I'd help. But I only meant to chat with him to see what was going on. I didn't mean for all of this to happen. Well, I did. He's hot. But what I meant to say was that I was trying to be good. But I'm an encantado, and this is kind of our thing. And then El Lobizon attacked and we were flush with adrenaline and that does stuff to you. I should know—I'm a biologist. Did I mention that I'm a biologist? Anyway … I am so, so, so sorry."

So she'd pretended to be me, and that's how she got to know Justin. I knew I should have been furious, but I wasn't. Somehow, knowing that Justin didn't know he was cheating on me and that he found out only afterward actually helped.

Then again, it wasn't like him knowing he was tricked stopped him from staying with her. She was gorgeous, obviously in love with Justin and sweet. I could see the appeal. And being the monster-in-the-night that I was, I couldn't justifiably cast stones. I'd done far worse than this encantado.

Far, far worse.

And then there was the whole her-imitating-me instead of simply seducing him by turning into some big-boob bottle blonde. I'd been around enough shapeshifters to know that they only assume the form of someone else when they admire them on some level. You know what they say: imitation is the highest form of flattery.

I was in a strange mood, which made sense. The last few weeks were hard. Hell, the last few years were hard. And Isabella, like me, was just trying to make sense of it all.

I grabbed one of the joints out of her hand. "Got a lighter?"

6

THREE'S COMPANY

*W*e stepped outside and Isabella lit the joint, took in one short drag before handing it over. I look at the red cherry, thinking about how it really had been about forty years since I last toked, or smoked, or took a puff of anything. Back then, I didn't feel anything. I figured it was my vampire constitution.

I took a deep pull and held it, summoning every ounce of my will not to cough. I might have not felt anything before, but now ... now was different. My head started to swim as a lightheaded feeling overcame me. Everything started to slow down. That wasn't quite right—it was more like I had more time to process everything. Like the world was operating at half speed, but my brain was working at full speed to digest it all.

"So," I said. "You and Justin."

Isabella shrugged. "For now." She said it in a way that made me think she was hoping to add 'and forever' to the end of that sentence.

"You really like him?"

"I do," she said. "He's different than most humans. He looks at me different than they do, but he talks to me the same as he does everyone else."

I got what she meant. Justin didn't care what color, religion or species you were. He was just one of those guys who liked everyone. But as for looking as you different, I got that, too. When he looked at you—really looked at you—you felt like you were the only thing he saw in the whole world. The only thing that mattered.

Remembering that about him was hard. It made me miss him even more.

"But, his heart is elsewhere."

"There you go again," I said, "with that brutal honesty. Most girls would be trying to play some game to scare me off or something, but you're all like, 'You still got a shot. Don't give up.' What's your deal?"

"I only speak the truth." She looked at me with genuine confusion.

"So you do." I looked around, seeking to change the subject. Enough about Justin. That would play out in time. "So, what are you studying here, anyway?"

"Biology." A flicker of worry crossed her face, her eyes darting toward the door. Weed-induced paranoia, maybe? "I'm working on a project to map the Other genome."

"You say it like there's only one. Aren't all Others different?"

"We are. But like humans of different nationalities and ethnicities, there seems to be one common strain. At least amongst the seventy-two species I've studied so far."

"Wow, so the gods ... what? Shared the same template when making you guys?"

"Not just us ... humans, too. The same four building blocks exist in all life. The only difference is that Others don't just have two strands of DNA. We have three."

"What else?" I said, genuinely fascinated.

"Excuse me?"

"You said there are differences. Three strands of DNA is only one difference. What are the others?"

"Oh, yes." She took another pull on the joint before handing it back. "Other DNA does not instruct decay like human DNA does. And, well, we cannot ..." She paused as genuine frustration washed over her. "We cannot reproduce. It seems the gods truly stripped us of our immortality when they left. We are slowly dying, and we can't have babies to keep our species going. Soon we will all die, and this world will be returned to the humans."

Her words hung heavy in the air. She was right. In time, every Other in the world would be dead, and with no new life coming through.

"Bastards," I said.

"Filhos da puta," she spat in agreement. "But I am working on a way. I just received funding from the World Army and—"

"World Army?" I said, handing her back the joint. "They're the same guys that turned Justin into G.I. Joe."

"G.I. Joe?"

"A soldier," I corrected, not wanting to go into the finer points of 1980s cartoons. "So the World Army is also into genetics." Government conspiracies and paranoia flooded me ... then again, it might have just been the weed.

Isabella must have sensed where I was going with this, and for a moment, I expected her to dismiss me. Instead, she looked around and leaned in close. "Yes. My research is about life. And they fund me well, but yes. It is troublesome." She leaned back quickly. "I shouldn't have said that."

Well, that was intriguing, to say the least. "Said what? 'Troublesome?' "

Her eyes darted toward me, and I'd expected her to look all stoned and easygoing, but she didn't. Not one bit.

I saw worry. Anxiety. Fear.

And it occurred to me that, only two nights ago, she'd been involved in a hell of a fight with those birds in the forest. And now everything was strangely hunky dory and back to normal.

There's a lot more going on with her than she's letting on.

Two of Justin's frat buddies walked by, and Isabella shook her head. "Perhaps that's a conversation for another time. When we're not ..." She held up the joint, offering it back to me for another toke.

Is that what people say these days? Toke? The last time I smoked a joint was in the 70s. That word worked back then.

Isabella laughed, and the anxiety left her face. "I think it's just smoke now. But then again, what do I know? I spent the majority of the last five centuries swimming in the Amazon."

"Five hundred years? You're an old lady."

"I am," she said. "But I figure once we get past two-fifty, we're all old."

I knew this was just an illusion caused by the marijuana, but still, I hadn't felt this feeling since being a vampire, when my brain really could process everything faster than a human's.

This wasn't entirely unpleasant.

"You know, you're right," I said. "Two-fifty should just be the new old. And we should be rewarded for reaching that age. I mean, humans get to retire at sixty-five. They get senior citizen discounts and preferred seats and all kinds of benefits."

"Yeah," she said, taking the joint. "They reward themselves for being old, but here we are—actually, really, totally old, and what do we get? Weird looks and ire."

"Ire," I repeated. "Good word." I burst out into laughter.

Isabella, taking a cue from me, also burst out into laughter as she handed the joint back to me. "English is my second—actually, fourth language. And of all the tongues I speak, English is the most cumbersome. So many words with double meanings, or that sound the same but aren't. Take the word 'two,' for example. You have 'two,' 'to,' and 'too.' "

She said all three words in the same way without giving me any indication as to which 'two' she meant. Not that it mattered—I got her point.

"Not like my native tongue," she went on. "Now that was a language. Simple, with no double meanings. You always knew what was meant. Always."

"Really? Say something in encantadoian."

"Like what?"

"How about 'don't touch my car.' "

"We didn't have cars, but I'll try." She lifted her jaw and started making some noises that sounded exactly like a dolphin chirping. "Ee eeeE EeEe eee car."

As soon as she said 'car,' the two of us fell into a laughter so hard that our knees literally went weak as we fell to our knees. I swear to the GoneGods, I thought my spleen was going to explode as I desperately gasped for air.

"That is friggin' hilarious," I said. "I can't wait to tell Egya."

"Tell Egya what?"

We both turned to see Justin standing there with a bemused smile on his face.

↔

"Tell Egya what?" Justin repeated, trying to pull off a casual look that said, *I want in on the fun.* Everything about his posture, however, screamed, *My ex and current girlfriend are bonding. This is a nightmare.*

Being six feet and change, he towered over us. And given that we were both wearing low-cut shirts, he had to work extra hard to maintain eye contact.

I knew it.

Isabella knew it.

But I wasn't entirely sure he knew it, because end of the day, he was a twenty-year-old boy with raging hormones, entangled with two girls older than his great-grandmother.

Relishing his discomfort, I didn't say anything. That was my motivation for silence. Isabella was also quiet, but why? I wasn't sure.

"Ahh, so ... it's good to see you guys getting along?" he said. I knew it was meant to be a statement, but it came off as more of a question.

"Oh yeah," I said, giggling. "More than getting along." I put a hand on Isabella's neck, and much to my surprise, she leaned into it.

"Ahh, so how's it going?" he stammered, clearly unsure what to say.

"Pretty good," I said. "I can see why you like her."

"Um, yeah. She's good."

"Good?" The devil in me was stirring. "What does that mean? Good like how? A good person, or good in … you know."

"I, ah, just meant that she's cool. You know. Fun to hang out with." He looked at Isabella with eyes that pleaded for help.

Her silence offered none.

"So, ahh, I thought that maybe we could, you know, talk or something—"

"How's your friend?" I asked.

"My what?"

"Your friend. The one with the blue eyes. He looked like he was freaking out. Hopped up on some designer drug or something?"

"Oh, you mean Rory. Yeah, he'll be fine. He just can't handle his booze. You know. Freshman."

I didn't know which word to take issue with. That he was lying to me about booze, or that he assumed freshmen couldn't handle themselves. I was a freshman.

Man, weed makes me mean.

Or maybe it just makes me more *me*. Either way, I had come to this party to make peace with Justin. That and show him how OK I was without him.

But now I just wanted to go for the jugular.

The thing about ex-boyfriends and getting back at them: it wasn't the jugular where you wanted to hit them.

"So, Isabella and I were talking," I said, pulling her in closer, "about the future." I put a second, suggestive hand just under her breasts.

Isabella was leaning in close. She was playing along. I felt oddly conflicted; I liked that she was helping me mess with Justin, but I also didn't like it.

Part of me knew Justin and I were over … and that he should move on. Even better if he went with a girl like Isabella. Sweet, kind, funny, pretty. But here she was, helping me hit the boy while he was down.

Justin's eyes widened with the possibility of his wildest fantasies coming true.

I took a step toward him. Isabella came with me without any hint of protest. Then, leaning in close to Isabella, I made like I was going to kiss her. That would get him going.

Because, at the end of the day, he was a boy with porn-filled fantasies, and I just knew one of those fantasies was getting it on with two incredibly hot creatures of the night.

Given we were both older than most buildings in this country, and he'd witnessed how differently we thought about things, he was probably thinking that this ménage-a-Other was going to happen. And just when he was sure it was a done deal, I'd walk away, leaving him blue in the face and his ... ahem, you know.

Only thing was, as soon as our lips were close, she leaned in and kissed me. So much for my plan.

"What? What are you doing?"

Isabella looked at me, confused. "I thought you liked me."

"No ... Yes ... Not in that way?"

"But all the possibilities?"

I gave her a concerned look.

She tilted her head. "It's just that when my lovers were confronted by their past lovers, things often ended with the three of us making peace with the language of the flesh."

"Making peace? Language? Flesh?" Holy shit, she was going along with it because she was a seductress shapeshifter who was apparently also into threesomes.

Shit, shit ... *shit*.

"Ahh," I said, embarrassed, "I was just trying to get him, you know ..."

"Blue-balled," Justin offered, an amused smile on his face. "It worked. Then again ..." He took a step forward.

"Ewww, no," I said, giving him a shove. "Look, this was a mistake. I'm sorry. I shouldn't have been so ... so cheap in my attempts at getting back at you. I'm sorry." I looked at Isabella. "I really am. I ... I got to go."

And with that, I made my way outside, where I prayed that some well-meaning bus would leap onto the curb and put me out of my misery.

7

BLUE BALLS AND BLUE EYES

"*I* am never leaving my room again," I said.

"But milady, you told me that your greatest desire was for life to return to normal." Deirdre pulled at my duvet. "Normal means going to class."

"I lied. I don't want things to go to normal. I just want to sit here and do nothing. That's not true. I just want to sit here and wait for death to take me."

"Are you still embarrassed over your welcomed advances? You should be honored that an encantado would be interested in you. In all the realms, their sexual prowess is legendary."

"Deirdre."

"Yes, milady."

"Not helping."

"I'm sorry, milady. Perhaps this will help." She yanked the duvet off me, and given that I was holding onto it for dear life, she also yanked me out of bed. "Progress, milady. Now I have picked an outfit for you to wear to your classes."

She held up a grass-green blouse with brown trousers that oddly went together. Progress, indeed.

"I'm going to have to leave my room, aren't I?"

"Yes, milady."

"But I might see him. Or her. Or both of them together."

"You might."

"What will I do if that happens?"

"What you always do, milady."

"And what is that?"

"Face your demons with indomitable courage."

↔

Deirdre got me dressed, and the two of us skipped breakfast before making our way down to campus for class. We had missed about five weeks in the semester, which normally would have meant that the semester was over. But we pleaded with the student admin, and eventually they agreed as long as we didn't miss any more classes or assignments.

I made it into my first class with two minutes to spare.

So far, so good.

I quickly scanned the room. No Isabella. Made sense; she was a biology major studying grad-level stuff. No Justin—thank the Gone-Gods for small miracles.

One class down, three to go.

The rest of the day was much of the same. Me nervously fidgeting into class and breathing a sigh of relief when I didn't see either of them. Day one, done. Only about gazillion more until I graduated.

Except day one wasn't done, because I still needed to get home. An endeavor that immediately presented itself with danger as I saw Justin standing on the steps of the Arts Building with two new buddies I'd never met before. Probably World Army cadets.

Luckily for me, he didn't see me. If I scuttled past and made a sharp left at the bottom of the stairs, I just might be able to make it past him without being noticed.

I hurried along, not too fast to draw attention to myself, but fast enough that it looked like I was late for my next class. As soon as my foot touched the bottom step, I breathed a sigh of relief ... too soon.

"Hey man," I heard one of them say. "Chill."

There was a grunt before a second voice exclaimed with a wee bit of panic in it, "Justin, let go. Please."

Another grunt, and what sounded like scuffling. *Don't turn around, don't turn around,* I muttered to myself, just before not taking my advice.

I turned to see the two cadets trying to hold Justin back as he clawed at the smaller of two. "Dude—what's gotten into you," the second guy said. "Let him go."

Justin didn't say anything. Instead, he lifted the kid up and threw him down the stairs in answer. Justin's eyes met mine, but they were devoid of recognition. They were also the same tinge of blue the other kid had at the party.

Turning around, Justin punched the other guy square in the chest, sending him flying back with such force that he flew over the stone banister.

Another grunt as Justin hit his own head three times before rubbing his eyes. A student who just happened to be sitting on the stairs stood up and tried to run up the stairs. He got three steps before Justin grabbed him and pushed him down hard. The kid landed with a sickening crunch.

"Shit," I said as Justin clawed at a second innocent bystander, and taking my *The History of Others* textbook, I threw it at him.

It was a thick tome, and smacked him squarely on the back of his head. Normally hitting a human like that would knock him over, maybe even knock him out. But Justin took it like it was a spitball, turning to see who was being so annoying.

When our eyes locked, he growled just before charging at me.

↔

. . .

Normally fighting with Justin involved some passive-aggressive snips and maybe a few swear words. But this time, he was trying to hurt me.

And not just hurt me—end me.

He attacked with a berserker rage, as wild swings and kicks came flying my way. Normally these random attacks would be easy to deflect and dodge; after all, I'd studied both aikido and boxing. And winning a fight against a trained opponent needed strategy. He had none.

But there was something more to Justin's attacks. They weren't just him taking random shots. There was a rhythm to his attacks. Fast, powerful and methodical.

He wasn't just taking pot shots at me. He was trying to take me down in a style of attack I hadn't seen since my time in the UnSeelie Court, where I had a drow mentor train me in something he called chaos fighting.

The idea was pretty simple: present yourself as chaotic. Wear your opponent down. And just when your opponent thinks they got you, you switch it up.

Of course, I realized it too late.

I ducked under a huge, overextended swing where he exposed his chest. A well-placed punch should knock the wind out of him. But before I cocked back my fist, he brought in his overextended arm and bear-hugged me into him.

I usually liked being this close to Justin, but right now he was squeezing the air out of me. I tried to headbutt him, but given the position he had me in, all I managed to do was ineffectually strike my forehead against his chest. Still, I could resist. Eventually I'd find a way out of his grasp.

He hoisted me up and brought down his own forehead, and I felt my nose explode with blood. The blow was powerful and disorienting. I stopped squirming long enough for him to lower me and resume his powerful embrace.

Justin squeezed. I could feel the last of my air failing me. I looked up at him. His lips snarled as spittles of drool ran down his cheek. His eyes burned with rage housed in an impossible blue … And by blue, I don't mean in that romantic way. The whites of his eyes were also blue. Just like a drow's eyes.

Our eyes locked as I tried to push against him, and for a brief second he loosened his grip and said, "Kat?"

Whatever spell he was under had wavered, and I wasn't about to waste the opportunity.

I pushed as hard as I could, managing to get some distance between us.

"Kat?" he repeated, the blue in his eyes dissipating like wisps of smoke. "What's going on? Why do you look so scuffed up? Why are you bleeding?" The last question was laced with true concern.

What do you say to someone who just tried to kill you? I just stared at him, using the sleeve of my far-too-expensive Burberry blouse to mop up the blood. He took a step forward, and unsure if he was going to attack again, I went into a defensive stance.

He was hurt and confused. Quite a crowd had gathered, staring at him with a mixture of rage and fear. My fear and their contempt was enough for Justin to piece together the clues.

"I would never … I couldn't …" he started.

"But you did," I said. "Bloody nose to prove it."

"Kat … I'm so sorry. I …"

"I need to know what's going on," I said. "This isn't you. This was never you."

"I don't know," he stammered. "One moment I was standing on the steps. Then I saw you trying to sneak by, and something in me just snapped. I got very angry." That last word came out confused, and he furrowed his brow. "No, not angry. I was indignant. Like I couldn't suffer the disrespect you showed me by trying to sulk away unnoticed. Then everything went blank."

Suffer the disrespect? Justin never thought like that. Hell, most humans never think like that.

"OK," I said, "we'll figure this out. Let's get out of here before the police or worse show up."

"Police?"

His two friends whom he had thrown to the ground were standing at the base of the steps. One of them whispered something to the other, who nodded and took off running. From the way he moved, I very much doubted he was calling the cops.

"Yeah … police," I repeated. "You just assaulted me. I'm sure one of these good Samaritans called the police." I looked around at the shocked faces, and even though the last thing I wanted was the police, my faith in humanity would have taken a terrible blow if no one called them. I mean, come on guys. Petite girl getting beat up by huge guy? That screamed 911.

"OK," he said. He reached out another hand.

"No thanks," I said. "I think I'm going to give you a wide berth and—"

I realized my mistake too late. Justin's eyes immediately turned blue again, this time with a snarl that reverberated.

He charged at me again with the same berserker abandonment, but I was ready. I'd pivot and use his momentum against him. Then I'd—

But I didn't get to use any of my moves on him, because Isabella ran out of the Arts Building and jumped on his back, stabbing him with a syringe. As soon as she plunged the serum into his neck, Justin fell unconscious at my feet.

"Oh, hello again," Isabella said, still straddling him on the stairs.

8

HOSPITALS, EVIL DOCTORS AND DEVIOUS PLANS

*W*ithin minutes an ambulance showed up. Good to know the paramedics were fast. There was still no sign of the cops, which was odd. I just knew someone had called them. Too many cell phones were out, too many fingers were dialing.

My only thought was that the World Army was suppressing the calls. GoneGodDamn their reach was far and deep.

At first the paramedics weren't going to let Isabella and me ride with them, asking who we were. We both answered, "Girlfriend," in unison, and the old paramedic looked us both up and down before saying, "Both of you? Man, I was young in the wrong era," he lamented before gesturing for us both to get in.

We rode in silence as they carted Justin up the hill to the Royal Vic, a short ride from McGill's Arts Building, where several doctors greeted us, taking him away on a gurney. We tried to follow, but a stern-looking nurse simply gestured at the waiting room and we knew we were sunk.

So, yay—I was going to spend the next few hours in a sterile hospital waiting room with my ex-boyfriend's new girlfriend. Another nurse approached me, asking if I needed help.

"Help?" I said.

"Your nose." In all the hubbub, I had forgotten that Justin had bloodied my nose. "We can get that looked at."

"No thank you," I said. "It's stopped bleeding and it's not broken. I'm OK."

The nurse nodded before handing me a flyer. "There is help out there," she said and walked away.

I looked at the flyer—it was for an abusive relationship helpline. *How can I be in an abusive relationship when I'm not even in a relationship?*

Isabella giggled, evidently listening in on my thoughts.

"What's so funny?" I snarled.

Her smile immediately disappeared as she lifted her hand. "*Desculpa*— Ahhh, sorry."

"It's OK," I said. "I get the joke. It's just that ... holy guacamole it hurts."

Isabella sat in the chair next to me. "Let me take a look." She pulled out a pin-flashlight from her purse. "It's broken."

"I know. I've broken it a few times as a vampire."

She nodded. "It won't heal straight."

"What?"

"It won't heal straight," she repeated.

As a vampire, my nose always healed within a few hours so that you'd never know anything had happened. I guess getting your nose broken as a human was different. I couldn't imagine my cute, perfectly formed nose crooked. "I heard you the first time. How do you know?"

She gave me a look that said that she just knew before pulling out some tissues and licking them. She started mopping up some of the blood. "I can fix it, but it will hurt. A lot. And given our past, you'll accuse me of hurting you extra on purpose."

I thought about my nose and how it was instrumental to keeping my cuteness quota up. "No, I won't."

"You will," she said, taking my hand and guiding me to the bathroom.

↔

. . .

"OOOWWWW!" I screamed. "You did that on purpose."

"See? I told you." She grabbed some toilet paper and wetted it. "Here, you're bleeding again."

I took the tissue and looked in the mirror. I couldn't tell what was up with it; all I saw was blood. "Is it straight?"

"You are a vain one," she smirked.

"Hey, not all of us can assume any form we want. I only got one face. Is it straight?"

"It is."

"Thank you." Tossing the blood-stained tissue away, I continued to look at my nose from every angle, trying to assess how bad it was.

Isabella started for the door, but before she could leave, I said, "What did you inject him with?"

"A tranquilizer," she answered without hesitation. "A powerful one."

"Something you just had on you? We were at the Arts Building, and somehow I don't think Milton 101 has tranqs as part of the curriculum."

"I carry these with me everywhere I go these days." She opened her purse, revealing two more syringes.

"Why?"

She sucked in air, debating what to say next.

"Why?" I repeated with more force in my voice.

"Because …" She shook her head. "I can't."

"Why not?"

"An oath."

"Oath? The World Army made you sign an oath?"

"No," she said earnestly. "Justin did."

"What? Why would Justin make you take an oath?" Whatever the reason, I knew that Others take oaths very seriously.

Deadly so.

Breaking one would be the last thing they'd ever do, and if they were forced to, they'd live the rest of their lives with a heavy shame.

She looked at me with pain in her eyes. "I can't tell you. I'm sorry."

But oaths had loopholes. They always did.

"OK," I said, "let me take a gander at this."

"Gander?"

"Archaic word for 'guess,' and not the point. Let me tell you what's going on. If I'm right, then you broke no oath. If I'm wrong, then you broke no oath. All I ask is that you let me know one way or another."

She looked at me dubiously.

"Justin probably said that you couldn't tell anyone anything about what's going on with him. But did he say you couldn't confirm suspicions?"

"Well, no."

Bingo. Justin was human, and humans were wholly unequipped for this kind of thing. I just needed to dig deeper.

"So here's what I suspect: Justin's being manipulated by that World Army cadet program he's in. Nod your head to confirm, shake to deny."

She hesitated. Then, slowly, gave a single nod.

"I knew it. Now, my next suspicion is that he made you agree not to tell anyone because there's some dark sh—"

"—sugar," Isabella jumped in. "Sorry, I used to work in a nursery. If one of the staff was about to swear, we were trained to jump in with an alternative word. You know, SH-ugar for shit, BAS-ket for bastard, FU-ire truck for, well, you know. It was important to do right by the children, which meant that not swearing in front of them was part of that." She batted her eyes as she spoke, and I realized that Isabella was being serious. She really was that sweet.

Sweet and kind and caring … and pretty. Arrgh, I liked her.

I hated liking her.

Also, she had interrupted me on purpose.

"You don't want to tell me anything more, do you?"

She shook her head. "I'm sorry. It's just … I can't …"

"I know. We're not friends, and you don't trust me enough to reveal the truth." I turned away in frustration. "We should go. See if there's any news on Justin."

We left the bathroom and walked into the hospital hallway. We had left Justin in his bed, writhing and growling like some rabid dog, and when we returned to where they had him restrained, we were greeted by a nearly coherent Justin.

His eyes carried with them that sky-blue tinge, but there was no murderous rage in them anymore. Standing by his bed was a woman whom I'd never seen before, stroking his hair like a loving mother.

I say that because she wasn't his loving mother. I'd met Justin's mom before. Well, *met* was a bit of stretch. I virtually met her on Skype video chat, where being miles apart with a screen separating us, I could still feel her "You're not good enough for my son" ire.

Not that anyone was. Justin's mom was super critical, not loving and such a terrible mom that she made my murderous, selfish mother seem like the Golden Girl of homemakers.

So, who is this woman doting on Justin the way his mom never did? I thought.

The woman looked at me and gave me a huge, inviting smile.

Huge and inviting like a wolf in Grandma's nightgown.

"I'm Serena Russo," she said, still stroking his head. Then she looked at Isabella and nodded with recognition. "Isabella. How are you doing?"

I turned to see Isabella looking away like she'd just been caught doing something wrong. Which was odd to see, because she showed absolutely no guilt toward me, given what she did with Justin ...

"Hi, Dr. Russo," she whispered. "I didn't expect to see you here."

"And what, not check up on one of my top recruits?"

So she was the bitch who was messing with Justin and the others, making them into super warriors. And I'd bet money she had something to do with those birds Justin had shot down a few days back.

Russo must have seen the contempt in my eyes as I put two and two together, because she said, unprompted, "I'm not the mad, evil scientist you think I am."

Somehow I doubted that, not that I said—or thought—anything out loud.

"Then who are you?" I asked.

Justin stirred and sighed like he was having some pleasant dream. I walked over to him and took his hand into mine. "And let me guess, this newly calm Justin is your work?"

"A mild sedative," she admitted. "Nothing more."

"A mild sedative to counter the murderous rage you're fueling him with?"

Serena shook her head. "You misunderstand—"

I put up a dismissive hand, turning to Isabella. "And you know this person how?"

"I ... I work for her," Isabella said.

↔

We walked out into the hallway to hash out whatever this was. Neither Isabella or I wanted to talk in front of Justin, in case things got heated and we worried him, or worse—turned him all kill, kill! again.

Not that he showed any sign of that happening. He was so docile that I doubted whatever Russo gave him was a simple sedative.

No way. I'd seen people come down from murderous, berserker rage ... They didn't do it like they were waking up from a pleasant dream, sedative-induced or not.

"So?" I said, letting the word linger as I held Serena's gaze in mind.

She didn't turn away—unlike Isabella, who seemed incredibly uncomfortable with Serena and me facing off.

"So?" she repeated.

"So what's going on, and how the hell are you involved?"

Serena chuckled. "Straight to the jugular."

I winced at this reference. As a vamp, I was a straight-to-the-jugular kind of gal, and part of me wondered if the reference was her subtly letting me know that she knew all about my secret past.

She laughed again. "OK, I see the concerned girlfriend needs an explanation. Justin was poisoned."

"Poisoned?" Isabella and I repeated.

Serena nodded. "Yes, we have an aqrabuamelu on the team."

"Aqrabuamelu ... those things are dange—"

"Dangerous. Yes, they are," Serena said, then narrowed her eyes as she examined me like a vet might look at a show dog or prized horse. "You're familiar with them?"

I nodded. "Half-man, half-scorpion. Babylonian creatures who were used to guard the gates of Shamash, the land of darkness. They're super poisonous, and their spit is acid."

Serena pursed her lips and nodded appreciatively. "You know a lot about Others."

"I ... ahhh ... am in Other Studies."

"Still," she said, "Other Studies doesn't cover everything, and to recall it from memory like that..."

Sometimes when you want to deflect a lie, tell the truth. Or at least part of it. "I have a good memory and I read a lot." I do have a good memory. As for reading ... I love audiobooks. That counts, right?

"Evidently," Serena said. "But did you know that aqrabuamelu have several different kinds of poisons? Some kill, some paralyze. Some give you one hell of a high. The trouble with the high, though ... the down often sends people into"—she looked behind her into Justin's room—"murderous rages. I'm afraid that Justin and some of the other cadets got Scorp to—"

"Scorp?"

Serena chuckled again. I was really beginning to hate that woman's laugh. "Scorp—the aqrabuamelu's nickname. Anyway, they convinced Scorp to give them a hit, and well, you were unfortunate enough to catch him as he was coming down."

"And now?" I said, nudging her aside so I could take a look at Justin.

"And now"—she emphasized the 'now' in such a way that warned me her patience was wearing thin—"I gave him a slight bump from

Scorp, just enough to take the edge off and not send him back into a rage."

Several cadets came marching in, many of whom I recognized from the frat house. "Dr. Russo," the lead guy said. I didn't know him, but recognized him from the bar fight with the centaur.

"Take him to recovery," she said.

They started in, and I grabbed the lead guy's arm. "Like hell you're taking him away," I growled.

The lead guy made the classic mistake of trying to elbow me. Given that I was a foot and half shorter than him, I easily ducked under him and used his momentum against him to give him one hell of gut punch. Right in the solar plexus.

He went down in a huff, and his two buddies had just started at me when Russo lifted a hand. "Enough."

The two stopped instantly.

"So, a student of Others and someone who can fight. You should join us."

"So, what—you can experiment on me, too? I saw what Justin can do. How fast he suddenly is. How strong he is. Don't give me the VR training bullshit that I've been hearing about."

Serena nodded. "You want the truth?"

I tilted my head and gave her an expression that clearly said that yes, I wanted the truth and, no, I doubted she'd give it to me.

"Fine, here it is. The cadets ... all of them"—she looked at the three boys in the hall—"are being given mild poisons from Scorp. The poisons are a nerve enhancer making them faster, stronger and more perceptive."

"Nerve enhancer? You mean steroids?"

"No, the venom makes the synapses fire faster, that's all. Much like nicotine, but more."

I turned to Isabella, who hadn't moved during this whole exchange. But she was looking at Serena now, so that was something. "Is that possible?" I said to her.

Isabella considered this before saying, "Yes, it is. But you'd have to isolate the active ingredient and DNA receptor in humans that would allow for such things. Very complex stuff."

Serena clapped her hands. "You really are one of the smartest people —Other or human—I know. To understand that so quickly. Amazing."

Isabella blushed at the compliment, and I gave her a light punch on her arm. "Evil scientist, drugged boyfriend. Now's not the time to go all gooey on me."

The encantado cleared her throat and added, "Not only complex, but also dangerous."

"I couldn't agree more. At first the cadets took the venom in stride. Their development was exponential. They had off-the-charts results and almost no side effects. But in time, well…"

"They got mean."

"Aggressive," she corrected. "But they only attack people who anger them. It is clear that you are the ex"—she nodded at me—"and Isabella is the new girl. And it is clear that Justin still has feelings for you, otherwise he wouldn't have attacked you."

"I don't know about you, but I'd prefer flowers."

This time Serena didn't laugh. She just shook her head. "Our experiments didn't work, and we need to get him back to our labs to try and reverse this—"

"Otherwise he might have a system overload," Isabella muttered.

"We won't let it get to that. We've already had much success with some of the other cadets who rejected the venom. And Justin … well, he was the last to show symptoms, which tells me that he's the strongest of the bunch. He'll be fine. I promise."

As Serena spoke, she literally crossed her heart, and when Isabella saw that, she narrowed her eyes. It was clear Isabella didn't trust Russo as far as she could throw her—and given the height disparity, I doubted she could even lift her off the ground.

"So, if you don't mind," Serena said, nodding for the boys to wheel Justin away.

"To repeat myself—like hell you're going to—" I started.

"No, Kat—she is right. The kind of facilities they have here won't save him. He needs other facilities. Besides, I'll be there to help." She looked Serena in the eyes, and for the first time in this conversation, she showed her backbone. Good for her.

"Yes, of course," Serena said, obviously not expecting Isabella's reaction. "We'll need your help healing him. Healing them all."

↔

A slow-burning rage built up in me, and I had to take three slow, deep breaths to stop myself from punching this middle-aged mad scientist in the throat. "OK, and how long will that be?"

"Unsure. It depends on his constitution. Anywhere from a month to ten weeks."

"Ten weeks," I scoffed.

"Could be a month," she said in a way that implied it definitely wouldn't be a month.

I wanted to scream with rage, but then the little demon in me spoke up and said what it always does in moments like this: *Patience, Kat. You'll get her in the end. You always do,* as the wheels of a plan started to turn.

"Fine, a month it is. But before I walk away from this pleasant exchange, I do have one more question. You're taking him because you have an Anti-Other poison ward, not an Anti-Other ward that deals with poisons, right?"

She rolled her eyes. "A common mistake civilians always make. You all think that just because we wear the uniforms and are mostly composed of humans that we're anti-Other. We're not. Look at Isabella here. She is one of our most valued recruits."

"I'm not a recruit, I'm a scientist that is technically employed by the university—"

Russo lifted a silencing hand. "And funded by us. We foot the bill." She eyed me up and down, her tone changing. "I know you. Have seen you around. Heard about your … escapades through the gossip mill.

You know, you could work for us just like Isabella here. She's employed by us, does her good work and we stay out of her way, and all of us couldn't be happier. She is truly brilliant."

"Ahh, thank you," Isabella said, clearly unsure if she should be thanking someone who basically said she owns her.

"We love this new GoneGod World, and we're committed to making it as bright and beautiful as possible. Isn't that right, Isabella?"

"Well—"

"You should read the literature some time." Dr. Russo pointed at a World Army poster on the hospital's local bulletin board. The sepia paper had the World Army's logo and motto as well as some contact information. Beneath that was a picture of several human cadets helping an Oni demon with his homework. "Can't you read? 'Making the world better, safer, stronger ... together.' "

"Humph," I said. "I see that. Thank you, Dr. Russo. You have been most helpful." And with that, I turned on my heel and hooked my hand through Isabella's arm.

The World Army was definitely into some dark shit, and I was going to get to the bottom of it ... in the form of coffee.

Foamy, latte-art coffee.

9
FRIENEMIES CONSPIRING

*J*ust five minutes' walk from the Royal Vic, Isabella and I came to a cute joint called the Dolphin Café. How apropos.

"Been here before?" I asked as we entered.

She swallowed, glancing toward the restrooms. "You could say that."

Another loaded response. And she seemed nervous; I could feel the tension in her arm, which my hand was still hooked through. This called for more than just coffee.

When we got to the counter, I stepped up. "Two vanilla lattes." I pointed to the glass display. "And two cherry danishes."

"Oh," Isabella said, "I don't eat sugar or—"

I patted her arm. "Today we're living a little, sister. My treat."

She didn't object further. As we sat down at one of the wrought iron tables in the corner with our mugs of coffee and our danishes, I leaned forward with both hands around my mug.

"Okay, dish."

She glanced up from picking apart the danish. "Dish?"

"Yeah. Talk. Spill the beans. Give me the 411."

"411?"

I sighed. "Tell me the truth about what's going on with Justin, the World Army and that obviously insane scientist you call your boss."

She sighed. "It's a long story."

I waved a hand around. "Can you think of a better place for long stories?"

She shrugged. "Point taken." Her eyes lowered to the table as she recounted the past few weeks. "It all started with a phone call from my professor. I had gotten funding for my research from the World Army."

As Isabella told me about the events of the past few weeks—the World Army's appearance, then the stymphalian birds, the murders on campus by a creature called Empusa and Justin's increasing strength and quickness—I sipped my coffee like we were having a regular old girly heart-to-heart.

Best not to draw too much attention to ourselves. By this point, I had begun to understand the pervasiveness of the World Army in Montreal. Who knew? Serena might have even sent someone to keep an eye on us.

When she finished, Isabella slouched into her seat like all the strength had gone out of her.

I set down my mug. Deep as I had been in my rivalry with her over Justin, I realized I had vastly underestimated Isabella. She had been through a hellish three weeks; I could only imagine the stress. "Well."

"Yeah, well."

"That's a hell of a time you've had. And why are you working for the source of all evil, again?"

She shook her head, eyes still on the danish. All at once, she took a huge bite of it. "Because mapping Other DNA will solve all our problems," she said through a mouthful. "Including the issue of babies."

"Babies?" I leaned forward. "Do you mean ..."

She nodded, taking another bite. It was like a dam had been unleashed, and she was taking out her stress on that danish. "Yes, I mean procreation. I mean Others having a shot at a future."

"Fuck. That changes everything."

Isabella finally met my eyes. "Now you understand my position."

I sure did. Between the oath she'd made to Justin and the importance of her research, she was stuck between a rock and a Serena Russo. She was trying to do good, even under a pitch-black umbrella of evil.

I set a finger on the table between us. "We need to figure out how far Russo has gotten with the gene modifications."

She blinked her wide, green eyes. "I've already broken into her office. I found a folder with a list of Others she's been harvesting, tweaking. But I didn't get to look at everything before I was interrupted. And then ..."

"Then what?"

"They moved her office after that—to the World Army's Montreal headquarters. It's locked tight as a vault."

I sat back, an idea percolating. "A vault, eh? As it happens, I visited a museum over winter break. And vaults have got *nothing* on that place."

Vaults-schmaults. We were getting into that place.

PART TWO

The figure came barreling down the hall. As she ran, I noted that she flailed her a hand a wee bit too much, turning her superhero run more into something a toddler does when trying to run as fast as they can.

Other than the un-graceful run, she looked exactly like me.

"Perfect likeness," Egya said.

"Except the run," I said. "I'm more Usain Bolt than Stewie Griffin."

Egya gave me a side glance. "Like I said, perfect likeness."

"Shut up," I said as I reached out my hand for, well, me.

My doppelganger handed me a key card before transforming back into her true form.

"What are you doing?" I said. "There's cameras everywhere. They'll recognize you."

"Once they see two Kats, they'll know it's me. I'm the only shapeshifter employed by them."

"Good point, Isa," I said.

"Hey, you called me Isa." A proud smile painted her face.

"I figured that since we most likely aren't going to survive this night, might as well die with a friend."

"Than a frenemy," Isa giggled.

"Frenemy?"

"What?" She looked at me confused. "You know … friend/enemy. Frenemy. It's a word."

I shook my head, amazed that an Other was teaching me new words. "Ahh, because you're combining the words together to create a clever play on words."

I'm not going to lie. My ego was slightly bruised by that.

Sighing to myself, I slid the card through the machine and it beeped as the door slid open.

"OK," I said, "Isa and I are going in. Make sure this level is cleared, then come meet us inside. You should be able to find us with the tracker."

"My nose is better," Egya said.

"Nose, tracker—I don't care. Just find us. We'll need you to get Justin out of here. Are you sure your contact will come through?"

Egya nodded. "He'll need a few days to sort things out. A few days that Isa and Justin will need to be in hiding … but yes, she'll come through."

"Good. Then let's do this." I put my hand in the middle like you would in a football huddle, or if you were a Power Ranger. Both Egya and Isa just stared at my hanging hand. I guess Others never watched 80s Saturday morning cartoons.

"Never mind," I said, bitter that my 'Go team' was denied.

Egya pulled me in close for a kiss. "You stay safe."

OK, not totally denied.

↔

The inner bowels of the World Army's headquarters couldn't have been any more evil, secret layer-*ry*. The far wall had numerous screens that displayed images of various Others classified in three ways: Captured, Processed and At Large.

In front of them were several rows of computers where the grunts of the World Army probably supplied field agents with data.

It would have been very much like a 1950s' military bunker if not for the surgery table sitting at the base of the theater. The table was surrounded by various medical equipment: an IV stand, monitors and a surgical tools counter. Typical stuff you'd find in any hospital.

But what made it especially creepy—outside of it being in what was clearly a military HQ—was that the table was surrounded by a giant pentagon.

I stared. "What the holy hell?"

Isa looked down at it. "It's a binding circle. To suppress magic should one of the Others wake up during surgery. It's standard practice now."

"It's creepy."

"Better that than an Other waking up and frying everyone with a fireball."

"I don't know about that. Where now?"

Isa sat at one of the computers and started banging away at the keyboard. "I'll download the data. You get Justin. He's in there." She pointed at the far wall, where two metal doors had the words *Restricted Area* painted on them. "He should be behind the door on the left."

"And is the aqrabuamelu still behind door number two?"

She looked in the tiny portal and nodded. "Still there and still dead."

"And still being pumped for all his worth."

Another nod ... this one more solemn.

↔

Leaving Isa to her hacking, I went into the restricted room. I had expected a corridor with several rooms on each side—you know, something that you'd find in a hospital.

What I didn't expect was one simple room with a single bed in it. Justin lay on that bed with two IVs in his arm, and he was wearing a pleasant smile on his face.

Interesting, I thought, *he's lying there like he doesn't have a care in the world.* Clearly he didn't know that he was covered in green scales and growing a horn.

10

ENCANTADOS AND EX-VAMPS
CONSPIRE

HE INNER WORKINGS OF ISA RAMIREZ'S MIND -

I looked at Katrina Darling, ex-vampire, kickass chick and fantastic dresser, with utter disbelief. "You want to do what, exactly?"

"Take them down. As in downtown … to the ground."

I was sure that last comment was some sort of human expression … and an antiquated one at that. We weren't going to take the World Army downtown.

But she was suggesting that we could take them down.

As in, destroy them. End them.

Obliterate them.

"How?" I asked. What I didn't add was that I was an encantado and Kat was … well, she was just a human.

I also didn't add that she might be reacting to meeting my boss, Serena. The two of them got on like a house on fire.

By which I mean, Kat wanted to light her house on fire.

And then, after our little chat, she was all about not only

destroying Serena's home, but also taking down one of the most well-funded government organizations in the world.

Remind me not to get on her bad side.

Check that … I already did when I hooked up with Justin. Remind me not to get any more on her bad side.

Still, she needed to hear my thoughts on her little plan.

I cleared my throat and, diverting eye contact (it was scary confronting Kat), I said, "The World Army is an organization that … it should be pointed out … has almost unilateral support among all the human governments in the world. They function way better than any other organization in human history: NATO, NAFTA, the Axis or the Allies, and the United Nations included."

"I know, but—"

Summoning an inner strength I didn't know I had, I added, "Destroying them would simply be impossible. Worse than impossible … irresponsible. Taking them down would only fuel their resolve. A resolve, might I add, born out of human distrust of Others. The attempt to destroy them will only mean that they come back stronger than ever. And hate Others more than ever."

Kat pursed her lips, listening intently. And from the way she carried herself, I could tell she wasn't just waiting her turn to speak. She was actually listening. Taking in my thoughts and considering them for all their pessimistic worth.

After a long, silent moment, Kat spoke my name.

"Isabella," she said, her tone harsh. She paused, and lightening her voice, spoke again, "Isabella—I mean, Isa—hear me out…" She walked over to her dresser and sighed before pulling it away from the wall. There was a small indent in the wall where part of the stone had eroded—I guess these old buildings needed a bit of structural work—and pulled out a cherub mask.

Scratch that … *the* cherub mask.

"Ah, I said. "So there it is."

"You knew?" she said, not taking her gaze off the mask. She held it like it was a heavy weight in her hands.

"Justin let it slip when I was pretending to be you."

"Ah." She sighed again—more heavily this time—and handed me the mask. "Yeah, that's me."

I couldn't believe that I held the Cherub's mask. This fighter was a legend on campus, having saved the dorms from a ritual sacrifice. And then there was the whole superhero debacle. And that didn't include the dozens of sightings where the Cherub saved students from muggings, fights and the occasional Other misunderstanding.

The Cherub was a legend, and now I was holding her mask.

Kat's mask.

"That's my father's mask. He was the first Cherub hunter. An order of monster hunters he created to stop monsters like the one I was," she said. "I took it off him when I ..." Her voice trailed off in such a way that she didn't need to finish the sentence ... but she did. "I killed him."

The pull of those last three words seemed to cancel out all sound in the room, like the words were a force of gravity that pulled every-thing else into it for what felt like an eternity as I processed what that meant.

She killed her father. And then she took up his mask. I didn't know much about Kat, but I knew she wanted to be a normal girl. A cutesy, fun-loving college kid.

No wonder the mask weighed so much in her hands. She was a creature burdened by two incompatible wishes: one to make amends, the other to live.

In my five hundred years of life, I'd often seen humans hampered by two conflicting desires. Those who found peace between those desires lived well, but those who didn't ... well, let's just say that graveyards are filled with humans who died with tortured grimaces from unfulfilled wishes.

"Why are you telling me this?" I asked.

She took the mask from my hands. "Carry the heaviest burden possible. That was one of the things my father told me growing up. Told me over and over ... carry the heaviest burden possible. He believed that if we all did that, then the world would be a better place. A heaven on Earth, if you will. But we must all decide how much we can bear. And that's why I'm not telling you to do anything. But what I am doing is telling you what I believe is best."

"They're too strong."

Kat nodded. "Yes, they are. And that is exactly why we must stand up against them. I'm not saying we'll win. Hell, I'm not even saying we'll survive. But at least we'll be doing something. And, if we're just clever enough we might be able to deliver them a blow that will set them back a few years."

"*Set them back?*" I narrowed my eyes.

"Yeah. The DNA mapping you're doing might have wonderful applications. It's also friggin' dangerous, too. In the wrong hands— and they are the wrong hands—it will be used for terrible purposes. We need to stop them. If not stop them, then set them back. The longer, the better."

She paused before adding, "I'm an Other. And I am human, too." She shook her head as those last words left her lips. "Humph, I guess Egya was right..." she muttered, and I couldn't tell if she was talking to me or thinking out loud. I'm guessing both, because she said, "I'm an Other and a human. I know how powerful—how dangerous— being both can be. We have to stop them."

"Or at least slow them down," I muttered.

She was right.

But that didn't make what we were proposing any more possible.

Or less scary.

But Yemoja, my goddess, never asked us to be naïve or stupid. Or weak. She taught us to be smart, use our wits and shapeshifting abilities for subterfuge.

She taught us to do what was right.

I nodded.

"And you must admit the venom and experiments on the cadets, the fights and random acts of violence that the campus has been experiencing ... that sounds like someone is trying to tweak human DNA, doesn't it?"

I nodded again.

A silence fell between us. A silence I broke with, "Heaviest burden possible, huh? OK, I'll do it, Katrina Darling. I will use my abilities to infiltrate the World Army and confirm their purpose."

"Let's go," she said.

I nodded, shifting to look like Serena Russo. Because I had done it before, I only burned away a few seconds of my life.

A small sacrifice to do what was right. A small sacrifice in order for me to carry the heaviest burden possible.

Kat was clearly impressed when she saw me do that, because her eyes widened and her lips parted with amazement.

"I'm ready now," I said.

"No," she said. "Not quite yet. There's still something we need to do."

11

HUMAN NERDS AND OTHER GEEKS

We took a taxi to a local home security shop to gear me up. Seems that Kat wanted to gear me up with some surveillance equipment so she could 'ride along' when I dove into the World Army's true intentions.

Part of me thought this whole expedition was cute. I mean, I was an encantado. Espionage and infiltration were kind of our thing. I knew how to get in and out of places undetected, how to seduce for information and how dig up dirty little secrets. I'd been doing it for five hundred years.

Kat on the other hand, was an overpowered vampire who could bite herself out of any situation.

But I understood her desire to 'ride along,' and I was grateful. However good I was at subterfuge, she would also have one trump card on me ... she was better at being human that I was. She could see things I'd miss. Especially in this modern, GoneGod World of gigabytes of data, cloud storage and emojis (I mean, seriously, do you really need to express happiness with a smiley face? Can't you just say you're happy?)

We entered the shop that was far seedier than I'd expected. I mean, it was right across the street from a strip club in a part of town that McGill literally gave us brochures for, outlining how *not* to go here.

This was meant to be a place where you got your home security needs met. Instead, I felt like we were in the place where Jesse and Walter White got equipment for their extracurricular needs.

And not to stereotype, but when the guy behind the counter has long, dreadlocked hair, nose piercings and a neck tattoo of a skeleton sticking up its middle finger, well, it raises some red flags.

Every part of me wanted to turn around and leave. But Kat walked right up to the guy and put her very expensive Louis Vuitton purse on the counter with a resounding thud.

She was sending this guy a message: I've got money and I'm here to spend it.

And from the way the tattooed man smiled, I saw she got his attention. *OK, Isa, take note. That's a move that will serve me well in the future.*

"How can I help you ladies?" he asked in a very heavy Quebecois accent. He spoke in English, evidently labelling us as the Anglophone foreigners that we were.

And Kat played into that beautifully. She leaned over the counter, doing her cleavage trick she'd pulled on Justin, and spoke in a Southern accent. "We're looking for a little something that will help us … ahhh … record things from a distance, if you know what I mean."

The guy licked his lips, not bothering to hide where his eyes were going. "We talking full HD, panned-out kind of recording? You know, for the Pornhub?"

"The Pornhub?" Kat said, her accent considerably less Southern and more Scottish. "Ewww, no. Yuk. What do you take us for?" Kat slammed her hand on the counter, pulling her purse off it like she was going to storm out.

At least, that's how I interpreted it. I was already at the door, holding it open for her.

He sighed, lifting his hands up in a defensive manner. "I'm sorry, I'm sorry. I just see two lovely ladies like you coming into a place like this and figure—"

"That we're doing porn?"

He scrunched his lips and nodded. "Can you blame me?" He pointed across the street at the strip club that, despite it being four in the afternoon, was thumping.

"I guess not," Kat said. "But we're not here for that."

"That's too—"

"Don't say it."

He shut up.

"We're here because my friend over there is going through a terrible divorce."

"*Quelle tristesse,*" he said, and I swear to the GoneGods he gave me a suggestive smile and subtle wink. "Maybe I can help in more than one way with that."

"Ahh, no thank you," I said, diverting my gaze. What was wrong with me? If I was in another form, I'd be all guns-blazing tough. But in this form—the form I chose to represent myself in this world—I was, sadly, myself. Shy and totally *not* into confrontation.

For someone who can literally reinvent herself on a daily basis, I wasn't very good at choosing more assertive personalities.

"Too bad," he said, turning his attention to Kat. "And let me guess, you want to catch him with someone else?"

"Seriously, dude, is sex all you can think about?"

"It's one of my best features." He stuck out his tongue, showing off a piercing. "Not the only place pierced for your pleasure."

Kat slammed another hand on the table. "Focus. She's going to have a sit-down with him, and I want to be by her side without being there. I want to see what she sees, hear what she hears and be able to feed her zingers that that will make his penis shrivel."

"Zig-gars?"

"Zingers. You know, witty comebacks …" Kat sighed. I, on the other hand, loved that he didn't know the word. As an Other, I'm often subjected to human expressions I don't know. To see an actual human suffering the same thing was … well, it made me feel like I belonged.

"I see," he said. "Zingers. Come with me." He motioned for us to follow him in the back room.

No way I was going to do that.

But when Kat grabbed her bag and confidently followed him to the inner bowels of this seedy, suspect place without concern or caution, I knew I had to follow, too.

I needed to be brave.

I needed to be more like Kat.

Still, getting killed in a place like this didn't really feel like the best expression of 'carrying the heaviest burden possible.'

↔

We didn't get killed. If anything, it was nicer in the back than the store front, with a plush leather couch in reasonable condition and a Nespresso machine that tattoo guy used to make us coffee.

Then he went to work, acting far more competently than I had previous thought he would.

He outfitted me with a camera pin that I could attach to my shirt, a tiny earpiece that, if I wore my hair right, would cover it up and a … "Wait, what's that?"

"A waterproof mic," he said, putting his hands way too close to my mouth. "It's so she can hear you."

"In my mouth."

"It's not like you can carry a mic in your hand, is it?"

"No," I said, "but don't the camera or earpiece have a mic in them?"

He shook his head. "Too small and too much ambient noise. This is the latest tech from Memnock Securities. Very useful when getting into places that you shouldn't be. Also very useful when dealing with Others whose super-powerful eyes that can detect this kind of stuff. Not that they're smart enough to notice. Stupid walking myths."

He said those last words like they were an insult. I had never heard that before, especially not as an insult, but I loved the expression—walking myths. That was exactly what we were.

Kat, on the other hand, took issue. "Walking myths? Like *The Walking Dead*, only real and mythical?"

He scowled. "Yes, walking myths—like they should be. Anyway, this tech is the latest from Memnock Securities, god bless them."

"Don't you mean *Gone*God bless them?" I said.

Kat turned, nodding with approval, and getting that little 'good one' from her made me feel like I was going to blush. Good thing I was an Other who could control those kind of things; I made sure my cheeks didn't rouge up with embarrassment.

"Whatever. They're expensive, but that shouldn't be a problem for you, eh?" He looked at Kat's purse.

"I'll need you to set everything up for us," Kat said.

"More expensive."

"And I'll need a van."

"Again … more expensive."

"And we'll need you to drive it."

"Tabernacle … That will be a lot of money, even for a rich anglo-phone like you."

"Oh, is that a fact," she said, pulling out a black American Express card. "Well, good thing I'm made of money."

12

LET THE GAMES BEGIN

I entered the World Army's labs looking like myself, Isabella Ramirez, my heart racing as I went through security.

The metal detector beeped as I walked through, and for a moment I thought for sure that they'd find the surveillance equipment hidden in the inner seam of my pants pocket. But the guards knew me. Well, specifically, Merl knew me. He was tiny, even for a dwarf, not that that meant anything. He was as wide as he was tall, and the softest bit on his body was his security guard uniform.

That and his heart. He gave me the biggest smile as he gestured for me to come over. "Hey there, Isa," he said with a big dwarven smile that was covered by his beard. "How goes it?"

"Oh you know, same old, same old," I said, forcing my tone to be even and calm. I might be able to control whether or not my cheeks blush, but it was much harder to control my voice.

They were two different functions, blushing more like an on/off switch than anything else.

But my voice. That was different—that was something that I couldn't will to behave one way or another.

I needed to be calm to sound calm.

And I was anything but calm.

"Sorry about this, but humans have their protocol," he said as he waved his magic wand over my body.

"Don't we all," I said.

As soon as the wand went over my pocket, it beeped again. "Something in your pocket?"

I forced a casual smile. "Oh yes." I pulled out a Twinkie and handed it to Merl. "For you."

He laughed as he waved the wand over the Twinkie. It beeped as soon as it was close enough to the tasty treat's plastic packaging.

"Thanks, Isa." He took the Twinkie. "You have a great day."

"You too, Merl. You too." I sighed with relief as I entered the World Army's Montreal Headquarters.

↔

Kat's voice piped through my ear. "That was pretty slick."

"Thanks," I muttered, trying to get used to the mouth mic. I stepped outside of the toilet stall, immediately regretting that I didn't pee before putting all the equipment on.

One of the things about being mortal: you had to go to the bathroom. Like, every day. Multiple times a day. That wasn't something I was used to as an immortal, mythical being. And sometimes I forgot to do it until it was too late.

Lamenting my missed opportunity, and too shy to do it "in front of" Kat, I resigned myself to a day of holding it and stepped out of the bathroom.

↔

The upper levels of the World Army Headquarters didn't look like a military base. At least, not one that I ever saw on any of the movies I watched with Aimee (but then again, we were usually stoned, so maybe I missed something).

Rather, this place looked like your typical office building, with cubicles and desks and people in conservative clothing and ties moving about with purpose.

Then there were the lower levels, where the labs were. And again, nothing suspect there. I mean, in the movies they make labs seem like high-tech, ridiculously clean, all-white places.

But the labs here were more of an off-white. And as for clean, I swear humans, with all their susceptibility to disease, sure don't take hygiene too seriously. This place was covered with the marks of dirt and dust.

The only place that was sterile was the equipment itself. It had to be if we were going to get real results, and I spent more time making sure my experiments weren't tainted with bacteria—or worse—than actually experimenting.

It was a real downgrade, actually, from working in the lab on campus. There, everything had always been ultra clean. Standards were higher, because the work we were doing was so valued.

But *somebody* (who was absolutely not an encantado disguised as Serena herself) had broken into Serena Russo's office on campus, which meant we'd had to relocate to the World Army's far-more-secure (and far dirtier) headquarters.

How I wished these labs were the puritan white of the movies. I would have mapped the Other genome by now if that were the case.

I walked to my lab and went about my business cleaning, mixing and testing while I waited for my chance to go deeper.

Deeper, through the elevator that needed a security pass to unlock. Deeper into whatever dungeon sat below me that I didn't have security clearance for. Where the World Army did their real experiments ...

But in order to get there, I needed a pass. And getting a pass meant stealing one.

Stealing one meant taking it from someone who didn't know I'd taken it from them and then returning it before they knew it was gone.

Which was exactly what we planned to do. But our plan meant that we had to wait for Serena to show up. And as I stared outside my lab window at her unoccupied office, I wondered if she'd ever show up.

Show up so that I could finish the mission and finally get to pee.

↔

Serena finally showed up at about noon. She looked tired, like she'd been up all night doing whatever people like Serena did. Her haggard eyes didn't even look up as I followed her into her office and saw exactly what I wanted from her ...

Her pass, sitting on the desk.

Part of me just wanted to grab it and run. But given that I needed to actually use it to investigate, I didn't think that would work too well. I needed to use guile.

Actually, I needed to pee.

"What can I do for you, Isa?" she said with the air of one who didn't have the time or patience to deal with me.

"Justin," I said, letting the word linger.

"What about him?"

"I need data, lab results, theories and venom to help with the antidote. I need—"

She lifted a hand. "You need to remember: you work for me."

I was taken aback by this. I had expected resistance, but Serena had always been nice to me. Respectful. Now she was silencing me like I was some minion or servant.

"See? She's showing her true colors now," Kat's voice said in my earpiece. I also heard lips smack like someone was eating a hearty meal.

Mergen—another Other I had just met today—was by Kat's side, listening in on everything, verifying the truth in whatever I saw or heard.

Yes, but she was always so good at hiding those colors. What's changed? I thought, not daring to share my thoughts out loud with Kat, lest Serena hear me. I also thought, *Something is wrong—very wrong—with her.*

"I'm sorry," I said. "It's just that I'm worried about Justin—about all of them—and I want to help. You said it yourself—I am one of the most qualified people in existence that *can* help."

Serena sighed and tapped something in her computer. I made sure to angle the hidden camera so that Kat could see the code she typed in.

"Got it," Kat chirped in my ear.

Then Serena pulled out a thumbprint pad and put her index finger on it.

"Shit," Kat muttered. "We can't fake that."

Oh yes we can, I thought.

Serena tapped at her keyboard some more before sighing. "He's under treatment below. Everything looks promising ... All vitals are heading in the right direction."

"Maybe I can speed it along and—"

Dr. Russo raised a hand, silencing me. "Isa, as you can see, I'm exhausted. It was a long night. My ..."

She cut herself off. But I'd been around enough humans to know she was about to tell me why she was so tired, and had stopped herself because whatever or whoever had kept her awake last night was her Achilles heel.

My knowing would make her vulnerable to me ... and Serena Russo didn't do vulnerable.

I should send her Brené Brown's stuff, I resolved to myself. *As a Christmas present—if, that is, she doesn't kill me first.*

"I'm just very, very tired—and as you can see," she said, conveniently not showing me her computer screen, "we're fine. I'll call you should we need you."

Kat sighed. "I've heard enough. Get ready." And I heard what sounded like a van door opening.

Then I heard the unmistakable sound of glass breaking in the distance.

This was followed by the van door slamming and Kat saying, "Drive. Now."

A French-Canadian accent responded with a, *"Mai oui,"* and I heard the screech of tires.

Two seconds later, Serena's phone started buzzing. Serena picked it up and looked at the screen in horror. "No, no, no, no..." she muttered as one hand typed frantically on her computer keyboard.

She looked at the screen intently as her other hand called up a number. I could hear whatever number ringing, once, twice, then a male voice picked it up. "Yes," I heard him say in a muffled, distant voice.

"There has been a break-in at my home."

"Understood," the male voice said.

"Hurry. Collin is home," she said, standing. "I'll meet you there."

Who was Collin? Serena spoke with the panic of a mother trying to reach her toddler before he ran into the road. Did she have a young child? It was hard to imagine her being a mother, but stranger things had happened.

Who knew? Maybe she was a completely different person at home.

Serena did a sweep of everything on her desk, including the pass that I would need to get into the lower levels, and headed for the door.

Merda, merda, merda! I needed that damn pass. *Think Isa, think!*

Then I saw it—her purse. She hadn't grabbed her purse.

"Serena," I said, scooping it up and following her to the door.

She stopped, and we bumped into each other. Hard.

"Here," I said.

"Thank you," Serena managed as she jogged out of her office, not noticing that when we collided, I had managed to get her pass out of her pocket.

13

GOOD, EVIL AND THE UPPITY FRENCH CANADIANS WHO STAND IN BETWEEN

I could hear the van driving as Kat's voice popped into my ear. "Did you get it?" she asked.

"Yes," I said, taking a seat behind Serena's terminal.

"OK, let's see what kind of bad you're up to, Serena."

"The password?"

She spelled it out for me: "C-0-L-L-1-N-!-2-3-!"

A very specific password.

"You know," I said as I tapped it in, "she's just trying to do what's right for her kind."

"Humans ... and they're my kind, too. What she's doing isn't right."

"I agree. But she's afraid. Humans are afraid. What would you have them do?"

Kat's answer was immediate. "Talk. Open lines of dialogue. Develop platforms so we can understand one another."

"Bold words for someone who wears a mask and fights evil," I said. "Not exactly the talking type, are you?"

Evidently my words did something to her, because she went so silent that even her thoughts were quiet.

I had silenced the great Katrina Darling.

That's a feat I'll remember on my death bed, I mused.

"Now we're going to need to bypass her fingerprint. You know a way," Kat said, speaking to our tattooed accomplice.

"I got this," I said.

"*Oui.* Tape on a glass, or have her touch clay or—"

"Kat, I got this," I repeated.

"How?" Kat asked.

"Like this …" I put my hand in front of the tiny camera so Kat could watch it transform into Serena's hand.

Not that she knew it was Serena … All Kat could see was that my hand had aged to look more like that of a middle-aged woman than the young adult hand I had chosen to have.

"People will see you through the office window," she said.

"What? A hand?"

"You can transform just your hand," Kat said, "and it will have her fingerprint?"

"The encantado's transformation is so complete, we even take on the person's blood type."

Kat let out an awe-filled groan. "Really? No wonder the humans are so afraid of us. You're like the perfect spy."

"Not really," I said. "It costs me months of life to take on a new form. But once I take on that form, I can transform into it almost at will, only burning seconds of my life."

"So you spent months to be me?" she said. "I'm so very, very flattered."

Sarcasm? Hard to tell with humans.

I decided to take her at her word. "As well you should be," I said as we called up Serena's files. Back when I'd broken into her office on campus, she had been a total luddite. She used manila folders and wrote everything by hand.

Now, that had all changed. All her data was hidden behind passwords, fingerprints and trees of folders. The World Army wasn't taking any chances.

At first there was nothing unusual on her computer. Just the typical stuff you'd expect from an administrator: employee profiles, time sheets, pay slips, evaluations.

Then there were her own experiments. Again, nothing unusual. I even found some information on Justin that confirmed what she said earlier to me: his condition was improving.

The anti-venom was working.

"It seems they are working on a cure." I looked up nervously from her computer. The way it was situated, no one could see me from the hall. But if they came up to the window and looked in … then I was done for.

My only hope was that everyone had seen her run out the door.

That, or her bad mood got around and everyone was staying clear.

Don't worry about getting caught, Isa, I berated myself. *Just get this done.*

I started copying the files, but there was nothing of any real importance here.

Kat knew it, too. "Shit, she must be keeping the good stuff somewhere else."

I let out an exasperated sigh. "I doubt she'd keep the files about her experiments on here. That info must be deeper in the lab."

Mergen smacked his lips. There was truth in my statement.

What we were looking for—her files, where the World Army actually was in regard to their experiments—was deeper inside the building.

Which mean I needed to go deeper inside to find it.

But once I walked through the restricted area I would be trapped. Nowhere to run. Nowhere to hide.

My only hope would be to get in and out without being detected.

I was an encantado; I was created to do such a thing. I took a deep breath and, ducking low into the office so no one outside could see me, I turned into Serena.

"OK," I growled. "Change of plans."

↔

There was no more playing around. It was time to act. I transformed into Serena completely and, grabbing her pass, went to the metal door. My heart raced as I ran her pass through the scanner and the system prompted me for both fingerprints and retina scans.

I got in without issue, and inside there was a long hallway that ended in a large room with several computers. This place looked like the command center to NASA, with row after row of computers and several monitors arching on the other end.

As soon as I was inside, I took a seat at the closest terminal I could find. Several technicians in the room looked up at me.

Well, at Serena.

I could tell by their gazes that this wasn't where Serena usually sat. I could also tell that they weren't going to question her. Serena wasn't one to be questioned and, as far as they were concerned, she could sit at any terminal she damn well pleased.

Good. This meant I could run through their system.

I tapped in her password again, and after another fingerprint and retina verification, I was in.

This system was completely different ... a lot more old-school, with Matrix-esque greens displaying everything. I wasn't sure why; we weren't running on an old machine. My only thought was that in the human world, some things didn't get upgraded for nostalgic reasons.

Kat must have been wondering the same thing, because I heard her chime in, "I bet its that font and color because the old brass got used to it and doesn't want to change it."

See, nostalgia.

Tapping on the screen, I started to look around the program. At first, I couldn't really find anything. Until, that was, I saw a folder labeled Project Chimera.

Chimeras were hybrid lions, bats and scorpions. They also had chameleon powers and a whole host of other powers that shouldn't run together.

They were the platypuses of the mythical world.

I clicked open the folder and saw several research findings that made my skin go cold.

I heard Kat's voice. "I'm no scientist, but are you telling me that they've already successfully spliced human and Other DNA?"

I shook my head. Covering my mouth, I mumbled, "Not exactly. Look here at this number."

"7:74 ... what about it?"

"That's the success variance. Basically, they tried to splice in Other DNA with seventy-four human test subjects. Only seven were successful."

Kat groaned. "And what happened to the other sixty-seven?"

I scrolled down until I found the word that answered Kat's question: *Terminated.*

"Shit."

"No kidding," I said. "And look here. Seems they had a second variance done, this time using the scorpion-man's poison. Serena wasn't lying. That venom made the test subjects more receptive to the splicing. But ..."—I traced my finger along the graph that went with the finding—"only for a time. Most test subjects rejected the new DNA after sixty-six days."

"Sixty-six," Kat muttered. "I watched Justin fight those birds last week. Did he display any powers before then?"

I thought back to when we got together. "Yes, last semester. On our first date."

Kat ignored my first date comment and said, "So we must be close to day sixty-four. He has a few more days, and then what?"

"Terminated," I muttered.

"OK, we need to up the timeline if we're going to save him. We need to—"

But before Kat could finish, I heard an 'ahem.' Looking up, I saw two frightened technicians staring down at me.

Clearly they had something to say to me.

Well, not me ... Serena.

14

EVIL IS AS EVIL DOES

I had seen the two technicians staring at me when I entered. I had watched them take deep breaths, and assumed they were so frightened of Serena that they would leave me alone.

But I didn't have the luck of the devil on my side. Seems the two technicians were only sighing because they had some news to deliver to Serena.

News they knew she wouldn't like.

"Good, you're in," said the fat, balding man with a thick red beard. He said that like he was trying to start up casual conversation. But he was so nervous, it came off high-pitched and squeaky.

The taller technician handed me a clipboard with a bunch of stats that, without context, might as well have been in Chinese (one of the few languages I don't speak).

"As you can see, the results look promising," said the taller of the two. Unlike his shorter, fatter, balder coworker, this technician was tall, thin and had a full head of graying hair.

They looked at me expectantly and, realizing that they thought I was Serena—who understood these numbers—I looked at the clipboard and pursed my lips, giving a slight nod.

Dr. Russo was someone who gave praise sparingly, and I hoped my tempered response wouldn't raise any red flags.

"But we have a problem," the shorter one said. "With the aqrabuamelu."

"The aqrabuamelu. Show me."

The two technicians nodded and started toward the far end of the room, where several metal doors stood with tiny portal windows no larger than a paperback. As we walked past the doors, I caught a glimpse of who was inside.

Justin.

It took every ounce of my willpower and restraint not to run into that room. I wanted to get to his side and hold his hand. Reassure him. Let him know that I was there for him.

The desire to go to him was overwhelming, and I might have succumbed had it not been for two things:

One was Kat. "Don't," was all she said, and it was enough. That single word carried the full weight of what was going on here. Don't go inside. Don't do anything stupid.

Don't mess up our chance to really save him.

I understood that I stood no chance at rescuing him. Sure, I might be able to escape myself or free him of his restraints. But he was gone. Asleep.

The other thing that helped me resist the urge to go to his side was his smile. He was obviously under a heavy sedative.

But despite that, he looked like he was dreaming about something wonderful.

And I hoped his dream was of me.

I clenched my teeth and asked in as neutral a voice as possible, "How is he?"

The taller one shook his head. "It is a miracle he's still here. It just means the other splicing took root. But he's slipping. I give him three days. Maybe four."

The shorter one nodded in agreement.

"What about a cure?"

They looked at me confused and gestured for me to follow. "That was what we wanted to speak about," the shorter one said in a whisper. "There's a problem with the … ahh … source."

As we walked farther into the theater, I caught a glimpse through the third window.

There stood the largest centaur I'd ever seen—even bigger than the one at the night club. But unlike Justin, he was awake and struggling against his restraints. There was murderous rage in him, like he'd kill anyone and everyone for the simple pleasure of it.

And he thrashed with the rage of a creature drowning in air.

"What's going on with him?" I asked.

The taller one gave me a confused look. "It seems that Others do not respond …"—he paused as he considered his next word—"positively to the venom, not like humans."

I pointed at the other door where Justin slept. "You call that positively?"

The taller one nervously adjusted his glasses. "What I mean to say is that the human test subjects are lasting longer and longer before the adverse effects of the venom appear. This is in stark contrast with Other test subjects, who immediately become violent."

"True," I said, nodding.

The two technicians immediately calmed down at my words, and I was starting to realize just how fierce Serena was. These two guys didn't fear her in the way you did when you thought your job was on the line.

They acted like their *lives* were on the line.

And they were probably right.

They took me into through the third door, where an aqrabuamelu sat strapped to a chair.

Aqrabuamelu are scorpion-man hybrids. Incredibly strong, fast and poisonous. It is said that a fully grown aqrabuamelu has a dozen or more poisons coursing through his body, each holding a different effect. With one simple strike of his tail, he could make you sleep, paralyze you, make you giddy, or outright kill you.

Several tubes stuck out of the aqrabuamelu's tail, with tubes running through them. I'd seen this kind of apparatus before. They were draining him, and I could only assume that each tube drew out a different type of poison from his tail.

That said, all the tubes were dry except one, and the aqrabuamelu looked more like a husked-out giant insectoid than anything living.

His dry body reminded me of when I was a child and would find dead insects. They always looked alive to me, until I realized that they were long dead, their hard exoskeleton still intact, their mushy innards long dry.

"He's dead," I muttered, more to myself than the other two.

The taller one nodded. "Died in the night."

"What?" I said. "But that tube is still draining poison out of him."

"We're … ahh … stimulating him. Keeping his poison sacks … ahh … alive."

"Like on a machine. Guess he didn't sign his 'Do not resuscitate' form," the taller one laughed.

His laugh immediately stopped when I didn't join in.

"Anyway, we can still pull out the nerve agent, but the glands we're using to make the anti-venom … ahhh, I'm afraid we can make any more."

"Any more?" I growled.

The taller one shuffled nervously. "Yes, but we did make a vial before he died. Enough to fully cure one test subject." He went over to a cryo-unit and pulled out a green vial.

"So do it. Fix Justin," I said, the words escaping my lips before I could stop them.

The look of confusion on their faces revealed my mistake.

"Yes," I said, forcing authority into my voice. "We need to know we can reverse this."

"Reverse?" the shorter one asked, narrowing his eyes. "We've proven this with the other cadets. Only a handful of cadets remain affected. Cadet 0088 being the last of the bunch." He gestured toward Justin. Cadet 0088.

Merda, he was getting suspicious. "So? Reverse him, too," I said, my voice firm. "One vial, one cadet. Seems perfect, don't you think?" I tried to lace my voice with the sarcasm I'd often seen humans use on one another.

They didn't move.

"Ahh, I see," he said. "Well, we're trying to dilute the aqrabuamelu's venom with neuro-inhibitors … We figure that a slow induction into the system should allow the test subjects to adjust better. As per your orders."

So that was what Serena was doing. Trying to use Justin as a final test subject … and not cure him.

Never cure him. That lying bitch.

"And is it working?" I demanded.

They collectively sighed, with the shorter one saying, "No."

"So there's your answer. Failed experiment. Time to move on. Let's fix him now before—"

"But there's only one vial," the taller one said, interrupting me. Not good. He'd never feel comfortable interrupting Serena Russo. He was onto me.

But from the look in his eyes, I could tell he still wasn't sure. And why would he be? The encantado illusion is so complete.

I held his gaze, and the shorter one, still fully believing I was Serena, stammered, "Ahh, yes, but … but …"

"But what?"

He adjusted his glasses. "But the problem … We used the last of the venom to make this and—"

"Can you synthesize more from this?" I asked.

"Yes," the short man agreed. "But it would take time, and that's all you ordered us to make."

"Make more," I cried out. "And then save that cadet." I pointed at Justin's room.

"But, we need to use this vial for … for …" he stammered, not finishing his sentence. Then he looked behind him. "And we'll need another aqrabuamelu to make more and—"

By this point the taller one had moved to the phone, lifting it off the cradle.

Kat chimed in through my ear. "Isa, you need to get out of there. He's on to you."

And that's when I understood. Serena planned to take the anti-venom home with her.

She was taking it for herself.

Not the other cadets.

Not Justin.

Why? Why was she taking it?

"—we're shipping it to your house today."

And that anti-venom was going to be transported to her home today. Once it was gone, it would take weeks to make more.

Weeks that Justin didn't have.

"I know what you're thinking, Isa," I heard Kat say. "Don't do it."

I couldn't let this moment pass. Not without doing my best to save him.

"Don't, Isa …" Kat said into my ear. "We'll intercept the vial en route to Serena's house."

And I had an illusion—a strong one.

"Isa, you'll get caught. Or worse."

He had such strength. I was naïve in admiring that strength—in coveting it. I wanted to be able to protect myself, to fell someone with a balled fist.

"Isa! Please!"

"No," I growled. "This might be our only chance."

"Excuse me?" the shorter technician said, a look of confusion painting his face.

"Isa … you're not trained," Kat said.

"I'm not helpless, either."

I heard a growl from the other end before Kat said, "Do you have a bigger, stronger form?"

"I once took the form of a sailor that I swear had bear DNA spliced into him."

The taller technician's eyes narrowed. "Who are you talking to, Dr. Russo?"

Kat sighed. "OK, we'll make a play for this. Do exactly as I say."

15

LEADERS AND LIARS

"*T*ransform. Now. And use their surprise to get the vial," Kat ordered.

For an encantado, transforming into a previous form can be damn near instant. We tend to slow it down because we know how impressive becoming something or someone else can be. We relish the expression of awe that paints an onlooker's face—the admiration that comes with seeing something damn near miraculous. And an encantado does love to be admired.

So we tend to do it slow. But we don't have to.

In an instant, I became that sailor. A man by the name of Malik Khillo. He was a huge man from Morocco, a man who had travelled over from Portugal on the Queen's fleet.

We had briefly become lovers, before Yellow Fever took him.

But not before he told me about the wonders of Europe.

Back then, in the late 1850s, I had taken his form and sailed across the Altantic to visit Europe on my only time away from home.

Well, my only time away when the gods were still here.

In an instant, I became Malik, taking on the familiar form of his hulking body, and swiped at the balding man, damn near taking off his arm as I grabbed the anti-venom.

He let it go without a fight, curling into the fetal position before me.

I had the anti-venom and considered going to Justin and giving it to him there and then. But the problem with anti-venom was that if I didn't give him enough, it wouldn't do anything but slow down the process.

And if I gave him too much … well, that was just as deadly as the venom itself.

I need to calculate how much he needed based on his weight and time infected. It was a simple enough calculation—all I need was a piece of paper to jot down some notes and a few minutes to figure it out.

But I didn't have a few minutes.

I didn't even have a few seconds.

I heard Kat scream in my earpiece, shattering any thoughts I had of going to Justin now. "Push the shorter one. He won't give you much of a fight. And grab his pass."

I did as I was ordered and turned to the door I had entered.

"No, too many guards that way," she growled. "Head to the back door. There must be another exit."

By this moment, several of the technicians had stood, their hands frantically pushing buttons that I was sure were a call for security.

I made my way to the back door.

"Get ready," Kat said. "I can hear two guards coming from the other side. Use surprise to your advantage."

"And?"

"And," she boomed as the back door opened, two guards entering, "hit them in the throat. Now."

My reaction was immediate. And so was theirs. As they entered, I managed to strike them both in the throats, hard, and they went down grabbing at their necks.

"Grab their guns."

"But I—"

"Grab them. Now."

I did as I was told, grabbing the two holstered pistols.

"OK, holding one of them in front of you, enter the hallway. More guards are going to be coming down there. As soon as you enter, fire four shots. Aim high. That should scare them away."

I pushed through the door and heard the noise of guards' boots. I fired four shots and the running stopped. Everything stopped.

Then the sound of running picked up again as three guards turned the corner of the hallway and faced off against me. They were carrying rifles that didn't have the 'let's tranq her' look to them. They were aiming to kill.

"Get out of there," Kat yelled.

I turned to run, but before I could take three steps, I heard Kat's voice again, "No, you can't run away from them. They'll get a clear shot at your back. Charge them, knock them down and keep moving."

"But ... but, what about Justin?" I stammered as the first guard took aim.

"We'll come back for him, but you have to move. Now!"

I didn't hesitate, letting her words spur me forward. I'd never used this body to run—hell, I'd hardly even used it to walk—so I was completely surprised at how fast I was.

Malik could move.

This body's speed coupled with his strength was incredible, and I nearly took off the guard's head. But killing him wasn't the goal. I didn't even want to hurt him, really. He was probably duped into working for the World Government just like I was.

But what I wanted and what I needed were two different things.

And now I needed to escape. I grabbed the guard and, lifting him with an unexpected ease, I threw him into the other two guards.

They toppled over like bowling pins and I leapt over them, charging into the hallway they'd come from.

I didn't know this part of the facility, but since I didn't recognize any of them, I figured that if they came from here, there was probably a security entrance somewhere.

But the hallway was narrow and the speed Malik's body had was limited in such a confined space. I needed to be something else.

I heard Kat's voice again. "There, at the back. I see a sign for an elevator," she cried out.

I started down the hall, but before I took three steps I heard the yelling of more guards. They were coming from a side hallway and would cut me off before I could get to the elevator.

I looked around until I saw another sign I recognized.

It had a weird symbol on it … not the typical male/female symbols you saw everywhere. This symbol had elongated limbs and wings—a bathroom symbol for Others.

I guess these guys were into segregated bathrooms.

But given that I didn't have the time to contemplate the equality of being able to pee wherever you liked, I leapt inside.

"Kat," I growled, "meet me the river's edge near where the pipes flow out into the canal."

"Where?" Kat cried out, her voice frantic.

"Near the shipyard. I'll find you … Oh, and bring clothes."

"What?" I heard her say, but I didn't have time to discuss anymore. I could already hear more guards clambering down the hallway.

As two more guards rounded the corner, I pushed into the bathroom, locking it behind me.

As long as I had a few seconds head start on those humans, I'd be fine.

But I didn't time it well, because the bathroom was, surprise, surprise, already occupied … by Merl.

The dwarf, unfazed like the human guards by seeing an enormous, gun-toting sailor in the hallway, immediately pulled out his gun and pointed it me.

I knew I had only one chance. I transformed back into myself and said, "They broke their oath."

Merl tilted his head in confusion as he saw my naked body before him. "Isa?"

"They broke their oath," I said, clutching onto the vial as hard as I could. I could already hear the footsteps clambering down the hall. The human guards would be upon us soon. "I need to run, Merl. Hide" —I held out the anti-venom—"and make this right."

Merl pursed his dwarven lips and nodded. "Hit me."

"What?"

"Do it. Punch me." He positioned himself by the door. "Now."

I didn't hesitate. I transformed my hand into Malik's massive hand and popped him in the cheek. He fell back against the bathroom door with more force that I had hit him with, using his body and bulk to stop the human guards from getting in.

Seeing how he was helping me, I did what I came here to do. I threw the vial into the toilet and, transforming into a baby dolphin, I made my way through the sewer systems of the facility, thanking the GoneGods that Other toilets had larger pipes to accommodate the huge passings of creatures like minotaurs and oni-demons.

This was my way out—as disgusting as it was—and as I made my way through the piping, I hoped that Kat would be there to greet me. And that she would have a plan to get us back into these facilities to save Justin.

But even if we did, things would never be the same again. Saving Justin would mean having to go on the run. Having to hide.

Very well, then, I resolved. *So be it.*

I was an encantado. Hiding was our thing.

Still, the future looked dark. Grim.

I wasn't sure what would happen.

But despite the darkness lying ahead of me, I was thankful for one small miracle.

Swimming here in these sewage pipes, at least I finally got to pee.

Thank the GoneGods for small miracles.

PART THREE

Katrina Darling Becomes Katrina Darling

I didn't mind the pain. The burning was a kind of cathartic release, freeing me from my past. I knew that I would never look the same. That my face would forever bear the scars of this moment.

But that was OK.

More than OK. It was right.

I was finally letting go of who I thought I wanted to be and embracing who I should be.

And as I screamed, letting the acid take its toll on my own flawless face, I thought of my father.

He wore a mask to fight evil.

These scars would be my mask. A mask that I could never take off.

A mask that I would forever wear, never hiding from who I am, never pretending to be someone else.

I was finally ... well, me.

He would be so proud of me.

And as the pain subsided and I got a hold of myself, I looked around the room, contemplating my options.

There was only one choice before me. Get out.

But getting out meant outrunning the bombs and, looking at my watch, I saw that I had less than ninety seconds to escape.

I would never make it out in time.

I finally got to be me, and I only had ninety seconds to enjoy it.

Oh well ... that's already more than most, I thought as I started to run. *Best make the most out of these last seconds.*

16
KATRINA RETURNS

THE INNER WORKINGS OF KAT'S MIND …

We found Isa by the side of the river, right where she said she'd be.

Or rather, she found us.

We had been walking up and down the shore looking for any sign of her, but in the darkness, it was impossible to see anything. Even with Egya at my side, using his hypersensitive nose of his, we couldn't find her.

Then I heard chirping.

Dolphin chirping.

Followed by the word *car*.

At the shore, I saw her transforming from what looked like a small dolphin into the form that I had come to associate with her.

It was incredible watching her transform … beautiful and terrifying in equal measure.

Beautiful because it was like watching someone grow into their new form. There was no ripping or cracking of the skin as it took on new shapes and sizes, no crunching or grinding of bone as it elongated to accommodate the taller body.

And it was completely dry ... with no moisture of any kind to be seen. (I think I would have been totally grossed out if she had been dripping with sweat or the body produced any kind of umm, shall we say, *lubricant* to help facilitate the change.)

Watching the change was like watching an artist paint some viscerally engaging masterpiece right before your eyes, and in the seconds it took for her to transform, I found myself drawn to her both with curiosity and awe.

But what terrified me was what Egya muttered under his breath as he, too, watched on with wonder. "Even her smell changes."

It was true. Watching her sit there, naked on the river's edge, clutching that vial, I noted that she didn't even smell like the river water or the unmentionable sludge she'd swum through to get here.

Instead, her body emanated a soft odor of vanilla—the scent of her shampoo. A scent that was completely missing until she became the person who actually used the shampoo.

And that subtle detail showed me exactly how dangerous she was. She could be anyone at any time, and neither I with all my experiences, or Egya with his heightened senses of sight and smell, would know the difference.

Even as I stared at her current form, I knew this wasn't exactly who she was. The encantado's natural form was more closely associated with a mermaid and a dolphin.

How can someone who can so easily be anyone ever know who they are?

Isa, now fully transformed, looked at me, and for a moment I questioned whether I had thought that out loud. But when she smiled at me with eyes that asked for my approval, I knew I hadn't. I also knew she wanted me to tell her what I thought of her little mission.

"You took some terrible risks there."

Her eyes sank. She had risked all to get the information she had and instead of rewarding her, I was scolding her like a child.

But I couldn't help myself. After losing Justin to his ridiculous risks, I couldn't stand the thought of losing another ... ahhh .... friend.

Shit, I was friends with my ex's new lover. Arrgh, the old me would have ripped out both their throats and been done with it. Being human is so complicated.

Whatever that confusion was, I cared for Isa, and seeing her in danger when I was standing miles away, powerless to help, had filled me with rage. The trouble with me and rage—I tend to share. "You could have gotten yourself killed. Then we would have had nothing to help Justin with."

"Katrina, girl, please," Egya said, walking over to Isa. "You did good. Better than good. Great."

Isa lifted her head as pride filled her.

"Don't mind her," Egya said. "She's not good at sharing the hero spotlight."

"I'm not good at tolerating risk-takers," I shot back.

Egya took three deep sniffs before saying, "Her odor is a mix of sweat and adrenaline. In other words, worry and the desire to fight ... to help. She was worried about you. And the girl, being so completely in control of her emotions, shows that in the most mature way she knows how—by berating you." He put a hand on her shoulder. "Trust me, this is how the legendary Katrina Darling shows you she cares."

I wanted to scream. I swear to the GoneGods—when I was alone with Egya, he'd pay for that. But that would be later. Now, we needed to figure out our next steps.

"The vial ... it will cure him?"

Isa shook her head. "No, but it will revert his symptoms. Stop the transformation and return him to his human state. But whatever they did to him has happened on a genetic level. Completely reversing that would take a concerted treatment. I'd need a lab and time."

"Neither of which we have." I threw my arms up in anger. "So let me get this straight. Justin is being held by some evil scientist in a secure military facility filled with guards, soldiers and genetically altered super soldiers. Whatever they're doing to him will probably kill him. But—and here's the silver lining, people—we have a serum that can save his life. If we can get to him. But even if we do get to him, we're not really saving him. We're just delaying death because unless you can get yourself into a lab and have time ... how long, exactly?"

Isa lowered her head. "I don't know. Six months, maybe?"

"Oh great, so unless we can get you to a secure location where you can lay low doing science-y stuff, saving him now will only delay his death. Not stop it. Oh ... oh." I snapped my fingers as one more thing occurred to me. "Said evil scientist is going to keep doing evil experiments. So as much as this is about saving Justin, our combined moral compasses demand we also stop her. Does that sum it up nicely?"

"Ummm, so very, very tasty," Mergen said, smacking his lips and rubbing his belly. "Desperate truth tastes like honey-covered strawberries."

"Good for you, Mergen. Good for you. So outside of Mr. Avatar of Truth, anyone have any good news for me?"

Isa and Egya sat silent for a long moment until Egya lifted his hand like a kid in class. "I might."

"I swear to the GoneGods, I will stab you with my dirk if you make some stupid joke right now."

"No, no," he said, his eyes holding a cautious concern. "Regarding the lab and time you need. I just might know some people who can help with both."

↔

"Know some people?" I said, drawing out my question more like a warning that a request for him to go on.

He lifted a calming hand. "There is this group of Others and humans. More like a network. They've banded together to help with some of the injustices of the GoneGod World."

"To help Others," I said.

"And humans. But yes, they exist to help Others who have wrongly been accused of a crime or who are being prosecuted for something.

THE HEAVIEST OF BURDENS

There are plenty of Others who are being accused of crimes they didn't commit and are now running from the law and need smuggling out of the country."

"Like the Underground Railroad, except instead of trying to get into Canada, they're trying to get out."

Egya narrowed his eyes. "A joke."

"You're not the only one who can be funny," I said, kind of hurt no one laughed at my joke.

"Yes, that kind of stuff. Except they're not about getting out of one country and into another. They're more about helping Others relocate to wherever they need so that they can live in peace. They're also about ..." He paused as he debated going on.

"About ..." I said, gesturing for him to spit it out.

"About preparing for the Other-human war they believe is inevitable."

"Oh great, so they're a militia gathering troops."

"No." Egya stood for the first time. "They just see what's coming and don't want Others to be slaughtered because they were unprepared."

"And what is coming, exactly?"

"Come on," he said, pointing at the laptop. "You have to see it for yourself. A war is coming. The humans are preparing for it. Think about all the technology that is openly being developed to keep Others in check. The clocks that measure magic use, the nets and super-Tasers normal police use to catch flying Others and neutralize super-powered Others. And that's just what we see. We also now know they're developing soldiers specifically to combat Others. The humans aren't stupid—"

"Don't you mean *we're* not stupid? Or does the fact that you can make your nose bigger now mean you're no longer human?"

Egya let out a snort. "Girl, when you attack, you always go for the kill, don't you? Well, guess what ... as hurtful as you'll try to be, I won't let you drive a wedge between us. Never."

He grabbed my hand, and every ounce of burning fire within me was doused by his unwavering loyalty and love for me.

113

"I'm ... I'm sorry," I said.

"I know you are, girl." He leaned in and kissed my forehead. "Besides, I can also make my nose wider, too," he chuckled.

From behind us, I heard Isa lean over and whisper to Mergen, "What's going on?"

"A negotiation of love," the avatar said.

"You shut up," I said, pointing to the pale white creature. "And you ... go on." I nodded at Egya.

"They know something is coming, and they're trying to ensure it's not genocide."

"And let me guess, they call themselves the resistance?" I chuckled at my joke.

Egya didn't laugh.

"No, don't tell me ... they really do call themselves the resistance, don't they?"

He nodded.

"Jesus Christ in a handbasket ..." I said, pulling away my hand. "These guys need to work on their branding."

"They're Others, Kat. Simple nomenclature and cheesy slogans *is* their branding."

"Humph, yeah I suppose. OK, this resistance ... where are they located?"

"I don't know."

"And how will they help us?"

"I don't know."

"And when will you know?"

"I don't know."

"Good. Glad we got that sorted out."

"Sarcasm is the lowest form of humor."

"And knowing nothing is the surest way to die."

Egya chuckled. "Fair enough. I will get in contact and turn some of my ignorance into knowledge." He picked up his backpack. "In the meantime, what will you do?"

"You mean the three of us? Oh, we're going to make plans. Lots and lots of plans."

17

PLANS, TRUTHS AND GETTING READIES

*W*e left Egya to go find the resistance and returned to my dorm room, where Deirdre sat on the ground sharpening her broadsword. "Milady," she said, not looking up as she ran the whetstone along the blade's edge, "I sense there will be a battle tonight."

She said it was an eerie certainty, like she knew tonight she would draw blood. A battle was coming. But not tonight. Tonight we were planning. I sat on my bed and gestured for Mergen and Isa to sit on Deirdre's bed. Isa plopped down, but Mergen just folded himself cross-legged on our dorm room floor. "Oh, yes, there's a battle coming, but not tonight, my changeling friend. Not tonight."

In answer, she continued to run the stone along the edge, a slow, menacing screech accompanying it. Clearly she didn't believe me.

"Can I see the building schematics?" I said.

Isa tossed me the flash drive, and plugging it into my laptop, an architect's blueprint popped up. "OK, so there seems to only be four entrances to the facilities—here, here, here and here." I moved to sit next to Isa and pointed at my screen. "But only one entrance to the lab. The elevator here."

Isa nodded. "Yes. But there is also an entrance here." She pointed at two parallel lines of dashes running along the edge. "It's a sewage gate big enough for a dwarf to walk through. The dwarven crew often use it."

"Ewww—why?"

Isa giggled. "Dwarves are not bothered by mud and sludge, preferring to stay underground. The thought of entering a building from above ground is a bonus to them."

"Fair enough. Still, they know it's not mud?"

Isa shrugged.

"So are you thinking we enter through there?"

"Or leave."

"And this dwarven crew. How well do you know them?"

"Well enough. They're my friends. And they do not trust their employers either."

I thought back to the affection the lead dwarf—Merl—showed to Isa. And when he'd helped her escape from the bathroom, Mergen had smacked his lips, which meant that Merl was completely sincere. He really would help with anything she needed.

"OK. So we have a disgusting way in and out should we need it. So assuming that we can get in, how do we actually get through all those doors? It's not like they'll be wide open. They'll need passcodes, fingerprints, retina scans."

She showed me her hand and I watched as the maze that was her fingerprint shifted. "That is Russo's fingerprint."

"Are you sure?"

She nodded. "When we take on the form of another, we do so in all aspects."

I'd just upgraded Isa from dangerous to unstoppable. Thank the GoneGods she was on my side—whatever side that was.

"OK. But what about passcodes? I don't suppose your abilities extend to knowing things about them?"

Isa shook her head. "It won't matter. All we need is a keycard and a fingerprint. There is no code. Not unless the system shuts down and we need to override it."

THE HEAVIEST OF BURDENS

"And do we have the passcode?"

"No, it is on Russo's person at all times. We would need to steal it from her."

"How?"

Another shrug. "I know where she lives. That's probably the only place she'll have it unguarded."

I narrowed my eyes with appreciation. "And you know this, how?"

"Because I have studied humans for five hundred years. Serena needs to be in control of everything, but she also needs to feel safe. Her home is where she feels safe. And that is also where she will most likely let her guard down."

I nodded. As a vampire, I used to stalk my prey by anticipating where they'd run to and how they'd try to hide. It was part of my method. Seems shapeshifters had a similar methodology. "Good enough. So we steal the card, break in and get Justin out. Still leaves us with one more problem."

Isa sucked in a deep breath. "How do we stop them altogether?"

"I would say something dramatic like we should blow the facilities up, but in order to do that we'd need explosives. And unless you have a dynamite dealer, we're kind of screwed on that."

Isa grabbed my laptop as a rush of excitement filled her.

"Hey," I said, but before I could get into full indignation mode, she called up McGill's Science Lab portal and logged in.

Once inside, she did a couple searches before saying, "We cannot make dynamite, but we can combine RDX, polyisobutylene and process oil."

"And?"

"C4. That is the chemical composition for C4. Well, not C4 exactly, as it will be liquid."

"Will it still go boom?"

"Oh yes. Very big boom."

"How long will it take to make this stuff?"

"Not long. Everything we need is in the science lab. An hour. Maybe two ... then we can—"

But before she could finish speaking, the lights went out.

In the darkness, I heard Deirdre stand up and say, "See, milady. Battle."

18

SAY HELLO TO MY LITTLE FRIENDS

*W*hen I signed up for the McGill dorms, there was this little box that asked if I'd accept having an Other roommate. Turns out that I was literally the only human to tick that box. And what was my reward for being open-minded and progressive? They put Deirdre and me down in the dungeons of Gardner Residence.

And by dungeons, I mean basement.

As soon as the lights cut, the world went black with only a tiny sliver of moonlight illuminating our subterranean room. When I was a vamp, my eyes would have immediately adjusted and I would have been able to see as clearly as if I was standing outside in the middle of a field on a sunny day.

But as a human, I couldn't see a thing. I swear to the GoneGods, how did humans survive, let alone thrive to become the dominant species with all these limitations?

"I can't see anything," I whispered.

I felt a hand grab my wrist. "Here, take my hand. I'll guide you."

Fae. Their eyes were adjusted for all manner of light, whether intensely bright or completely absent.

"No Deirdre, we're under attack. I'm going to need you free and nimble to, umm, dispatch the enemy."

"Milady?" I heard her say from the hallway. "What are you—?"

There was a shuffle as Deirdre said, "What manner of dark magic is this? Unhand milady."

"What?" And then it hit me: Isabella could shapeshift. And she was an Other specialist. Combine those two things and I understood exactly what was happening.

She had shifted into Deirdre's form ... in other words, an Other who could see in the dark. Which meant she had just burnt months off her life to take on Deirdre's form.

GoneGodDamn, that was fast. And an expensive sacrifice of her life.

I guess if there was ever a time to make such a sacrifice, now was that time. The lights were gone, and I was pretty sure I knew why.

"Deirdre. As in, real Deirdre," I corrected. "Isa is an ally, and she's just trying to help."

Deirdre growled, and I could sense that she took another step forward before audibly sighing and saying, "It is strange to look into a mirror that does not move like you do. Take care of her well, shifter, for if not, I swear to the GoneGods that once I am done with these foes, I will come for you."

"I swear by everything I hold holy and true, I will do whatever is in my power to protect her," Deirdre—or rather, Isabella—said. It was all so confusing. She spoke with the exact same Irish lilt as the real changeling.

"Fine. Good we got all those oaths and promises out of the way. Mergen ... can you see in the dark?"

The Avatar of Truth smacked his lips. "I can see the truth ... and the truth of your purpose lights my way."

"So, yes?"

I don't know what expression Mergen wore when he answered. I could only imagine it was one of defeat and frustration at me not accepting his truth-of-your-purpose explanation, because he responded with a deflated, "Yes," and nothing more.

"Good. So here's the mission objective ..." *Mission objective.* Look at me speaking all militarily. Justin wasn't the only one who could do that. "We have to assume that this is the World Army coming after us. Either that or some random baddie—which, to be honest, I'm not willing to accept. I can only deal with one evil at a time. So, we need to get out of here. But we can't just leave. First of all, they're probably watching the exits. And secondly, there are a lot of innocents here."

"So what do we do?"

"First, I need one of you can-see-in-the-dark beings to grab my mask and dirk. Then Deirdre and I say goodbye to our home. We're never coming back here again."

A hand reached for mine and I could feel the dirk and my father's mask slip into mine. "Now what?" Deirdre asked.

"Now, we hurt them bad. *Hurt them,*" I repeated in the direction I believed Deirdre was standing, "not kill them. They're human, after all. We make them pay a price for coming after us. Then we run. Isabella, can we break into the labs today and mix the C4?"

"It's not exactly C4. It's—"

"Can we make things that go boom tonight?"

"If I can get to my lab, yes."

"Good. So tonight's to-do list is: kick some human army ass, make bombs, rescue Justin and blow things up. Let's get to it."

↔

The thing about to-do lists: some items simply refuse to get crossed off. We left my room, Isabella guiding me through the darkness with her borrowed changeling eyes.

How much time did she burn to shift? For one so willing to run away, she had no issue using magic and shortening her life. I could have dismissed this as her simply wanting to escape. But if that were true, she would have shifted into some random student's image and disappeared in the chaos.

And as much as I knew we were becoming besties—not—I don't think saving me was high on her priority list. Which left only one motivation that made sense.

She wanted to save Justin and needed me to do it.

GoneGodDamn, she loved the boy.

Time to let him go, I thought.

"Let who go?" Isabella whispered.

"Nothing. I was just thinking that … You know what, it can wait. Let's survive the evening and I'll think my thoughts out loud on purpose. What do you see?"

I heard the shuffling of the three Others as we grouped together in the basement hallway.

"Nothing," Isabella said. "The hall is empty. One kid—"

"Harold," Deirdre offered.

"—stuck his head out of his room, looked around and when he couldn't see anything, went back inside. Other than that, nothing."

"What the hell are they doing?"

"Maybe it's just a power cut?"

I shook my head, not that anyone could see it. "No, we're on the same power grid as the Royal Vic. There are backup generators that kick in should we lose power. A few minutes, maybe. But this long? No way. It's them."

Isabella turned to me. "You speak with such confidence."

She said it not in a critical, questioning way, but rather with admiration. Like she'd never known anyone to 'just know' things. Made sense. She was a creature that relied on guile and subterfuge to survive. You only got that way when you questioned everything, trying to come up with plans that covered the greatest number of possibilities.

"Let's go," I said.

We took a few steps forward before we heard a buzzing that sounded like four mini-fans. "What the fresh hell?" I said.

"Milady," Deirdre said, "a children's toy just flew in the hallway."

"Children's toy? No, that's a drone. Shit—kill it."

"The toy?"

"Yes, the toy," I said frantically.

Deirdre didn't hesitate, darting forward and felling the drone with one clanking stroke of her broadsword. I heard two plastic clumps hit the ground.

"OK, so they know where we are. There's only two exits, the stairs and fire exit."

"The elevator," Isabella said.

"I don't know about you, but I don't want to be trapped in a box where we can be shot like fish in a barrel. Or box. Whatever."

"The power is out."

"So?"

"So that means that the elevator's doors are unlocked. It's a safety protocol so people don't get trapped inside. We can climb the shaft without fear of being crushed by someone waiting on the ground floor."

Subterfuge and guile. I like it.

"OK, let's go."

↔

We made our way to the elevator shaft. Well, *they* made their way to the elevator shaft. I played the role of helpless human—it was humiliating, and oddly comforting. Was that what the people I'd ferried to safety felt? A mixture of gratitude and utter frustration? If that was so, then I really needed to work on my 'inclusive' game when helping.

"Over here," one of the Deirdres said, and I heard powerful arms force apart the locked elevator doors with barely a grunt of effort. GoneGodDamn she was strong. Safety protocols locked those doors during a power outage to stop people from doing exactly what we wanted to do.

I guess safety protocols didn't take into account changeling strength.

Mergen muttered something to himself.

"Come again?" I said.

I felt the Avatar of Truth's hot breath on the back of my neck as he repeated what he had said, "This is the end."

Given that he was a being who could literally sense the truth and had prophetic qualities to his essence, I kind of wished I hadn't asked.

Then again, he wasn't saying anything I didn't already know. As soon as those lights cut, I knew my home here was done. It was one thing being stalked by deadly enemies and nefarious Others. Being hunted by the government ... that was something else entirely.

Something I'd have to figure out later. After I survived the elevator shaft.

If I survived the elevator shaft.

"Milady, this way." Deirdre—the real Deirdre—guided me to the opening. "I can carry you, if—"

"No, I'll be fine. I managed to shimmy down the decaying blouse of a dead goddess," I muttered as I felt around for something to grab onto for my ascent.

"What?" Isa said.

"Nothing—just what I was up to over Christmas break. You know, eggnog, turkeys and dead gods. You?"

"Ahh, I was on campus working—"

"It was a rhetorical question."

"Oh yes, of course." I couldn't see her face, but I like to think that her Deirdre-borrowed cheeks flushed red. OK, so the demon in me wasn't totally over her stealing my boyfriend.

"Here goes nothing," I said, and fumbled about until I found the steel track that the elevator carriage's rollers used. Gripping both sides, I started to climb up.

↔

. . .

We must have managed to get up three flights before two things happened almost in sync. One, we found the elevator dead in the shaft. Two, a tiny drone made its way into the tube of machine grease and metal. The sound of the drone was unmistakable—four little fans frantically spinning as it flew inside to get a fix on our location.

But almost as quickly as the drone entered, I heard a crash as Deirdre or Mergen (or maybe Isabella) threw something at it, destroying it instantly.

"Nice shot."

"Ummm, indeed," Mergen said.

"Thank you, milady." Deirdre's voice was strained as she pushed against the elevator's trap door, opening the path in.

Inside the carriage, I took a deep breath before saying, "OK, they know we're in here. We either keep going up or we make a break here."

"I cannot hear them or their tiny flying dragons in the hall," Deirdre said.

"So we make a break for it. Let's go before they have to a chance to catch up."

"Once in the hall, then what?"

Then what, indeed. "We need to break through their line of defense." I could hear Deirdre pulling apart the doors like Moses parting the Red Sea. OK, I'm sure it was nothing so dramatic, but I still liked the imagery. "Once we're in the hall, run to the central stair- well. Let's see if we can catch some of them off guard and—"

But before I could finish the thought, two strings of blue, electric lighting shot across the hall, illuminating both their path and Deirdre. She was being tazed. Not just tazed; the crackling energy was more than any standard-issue Taser could do.

She was being electrocuted.

I immediately swung my dirk downward, severing the lines and grabbing them.

Without connecting to a body, the lines had no power to them and any light they provided was gone. They did, however, offer me a direct line to whomever shot it. I pulled at the wires as I made my way down the hall as fast as I could until I found a body to associate with it. I was fast—faster than these two could anticipate—and I immediately took down the soldier on the left as Mergen charged at the other one.

"Two down," I said as a flashlight shone in my face.

Shit—more soldiers. I braced myself for another Taser or worse, but instead of feeling any pain, I heard a voice say, "It's you. The Cherub."

A student had come out of their room to see what was going on.

"Please, get back in your room," I said. "We're under attack. You'll be safe inside."

"Attack? Who?"

I didn't answer, moving toward the light and pushing him inside. From his bulk, I knew he was an Other. Perhaps the oni demon who lived on the third floor. Or maybe the valkyrie.

"Please. Get inside." And raising my voice—no point in hiding; they knew where we were—said, "Everyone, please stay inside. I am sorry for bringing this to your doorstep. But these people ... they are after me. Not you. You will be safe as long as you stay out of the way."

"The Cherub, she lives in Gardner Hall?" I heard someone say.

"I knew she was one of us. No way someone who moves like that could be part of Molson or the other dorms."

There was a cheer of residential pride, and for a brief second I reveled in it. Hey, I might be under attack, but a girl can still enjoy a wee bit of positivity, can't she?

"Get inside. Please." Then, whistling for the others to join me, I gestured for them to follow. "Deirdre—you OK?" I asked.

The changeling groaned in response. "I was once doused with the full brunt of a silver dragon's electric breath weapon. That hurt more."

"Good to know," I said. "Let's go."

19

NO WAY OUT

We made our way to the central stairwell, but not before I disarmed the two soldiers of their Tasers and batons. The central stairwell ran along the side of the building with windows lining it. Moonlight illuminated the area slightly, which meant that they didn't just cut the power to Gardner Hall, but the entire hill. A hill that also had a hospital on it.

I shuddered to think that patients were suffering because these assholes wanted to take us down.

But they couldn't turn off the moon, and from the little lighting it offered I could see the hillside teeming with soldiers. At least two dozen by my count, which meant there were probably a dozen more.

Fighting our way out of this wasn't going to happen. They were all lying down, rifles out in a typical don't-disclose-your-position manner.

Only one of them seemed to be out in the open—a non-human in army fatigues. From this distance I couldn't tell what kind of Other he was. The creature was standing way off in the distance and his hands moved in front of his chest like he was playing with an invisible ball or something.

I'd seen that kind of hand gesturing before. With witches.

Our best hope was getting behind the building and into the forested area surrounding the dorms. At least there we had a chance of losing them.

"Isabella, maybe you should do one of your shapeshifter tricks and go hide in someone's room?"

Isabella shook her head.

"Come on, now's not the time to be brave. Besides, once we draw them away, you can go to your lab and make the C4."

"I don't think I can hide easily."

"Why not? You can literally look like anyone you want."

"True, but they found us. Here."

"So?"

"I have been shifting for the purposes of hiding for centuries. They did not track me. Which meant that they have other ways to find me."

I shook my head. "Like what? A tracker device?"

"Maybe. Probably. But where it would be, I do not know." She pursed her lips and shook her head. "Besides, Justin's only hope is that we escape and carry out our plan. Tonight."

Her face wore the kind of bravery that came from one who wanted nothing more than to run, but despite her fear, was choosing to stay.

She was right.

She was being tracked, but how?

I remembered the strange Other who was rubbing that invisible ball and a terrible thought occurred to me. I grabbed a pair of goggles off one of the soldiers I'd taken down and put them on, and while I saw the expected night vision's green hues illuminating my surroundings, I also saw a small screen on the upper right-hand corner with an image of Isabella. She was marked in red and stood alone, even though we were right next to her.

"Isabella, did you sign an NDA when you began working with the World Army?"

A pause. "Well, in a manner of speaking. How did you know?"

I ignored her question. "When you signed that NDA, was there anything strange and or magical about it?"

Isabella thought about it before saying, "I never signed it. I had to give them a droplet of blood, though, to bind the contract."

"You know that humans use ink ... from a pen."

The expression on her face clearly indicated that she didn't.

"Shit, you're right—they are tracking you. With magic. See that guy over there? He's some kind of shaman."

Isabella looked out across the field. "That's Kendall. He's a wendigo shaman."

"Yay. You couldn't hide if you wanted to. OK, so the plan just got more complicated. Not only do we need to get away and hide, we need to take out tracer-witch there in order to stay hidden. You'll need this." I handed her the Taser.

"I don't know how to use this."

"It's easy. Just point and shoot."

Isa nodded.

"But making our stand and fighting our way out of this ... I don't see that happening. There are too many of them. They have this place surrounded."

Mergen smacked his lips in anticipation. "So true."

"Not helping, dude," I said.

"Indeed," he said as he licked his fingers in the that-was-good-barbeque kind of way.

"We're only on the third floor. Maybe we could get out a window and—" Isabella started.

"They'll have the back covered, too," I said.

Deirdre stood. "Then I will clear a path. It will be my greatest honor."

"No, Deirdre, I'm not losing you to this." Brave words, given I might not have a choice in this. My brain raced with every possible scenario I could think of for escape, desperately trying to come up with a plan.

But any hopes of a plan were dashed with the crackling of the downed soldier's radio.

↔

The radio crackled again. I knew I shouldn't be drawn to it, that I should just let it call out to the oblivion, but I was spurred on by curiosity and the hope that if I spoke to these assholes I'd see a way out of this. How big was my ego that I thought I'd be able to negotiate with them? Or out-smart them …

Sometimes I am humbled by my own arrogance.

I picked up the radio and put it to my ear. I don't know if there was a sensor or another drone, but as soon as the earpiece was in place, I heard a familiar voice say, "Katrina Darling."

"Serena Russo, I presume."

"Katrina Darling, nineteen-year-old human with virtually no social media presence, a forged birth certificate and passports. It didn't take much digging to figure out who you really are."

"And?"

"Three-hundred-year-old vampire, the daughter Eoghan McMahon, inspiration for the Order of Divine Cherub Hunters and a murderous bitch."

"Ouch," I said, "no need to get personal. And what do you want, exactly? A cookie? A medal? All that shit was figured out already by the Diamond Dogs."

"The Diamond Dogs?" she said, less of a question and more a surprise that I even knew that name.

"You know, General Shouf's division," I said, seeing a possible way out of this. "A few weeks back I helped them out by killing three dead gods. And before you ask, yes, dead gods need to be killed twice."

There was silence as I presumed she was checking it out.

Maybe, just maybe, she'd see my connection to that event and her searches would trigger some kind of red flag or something.

Then General Shouf and Jean could swoop in and save us from this hell. Of course, General Shouf would want to make me one of her operatives, so being rescued by her would be something akin to 'out of the fire and into the frying pan' ... or whatever the expression was.

After an agonizing minute, the radio crackled. "Interesting. It says here that you died in that assault. I'm guessing that was your reward? Death—at least as far as the world is concerned. Whatever the reason for this clerical error, it will make what I'm going to do to you much easier to clean up."

OK, so that backfired.

"Listen, you—"

"Let me spare you the superhero speech and make this easy for you. Surrender."

"No," I said.

"Hold on. Let me finish. I have a whole carrot-stick routine prepared to entice you."

I walked over to the window, and in the field I saw Serena emerge and walk to the center of the quad. She waved at me like we were friends meeting for a coffee or something.

"OK," I said, "I'm listening. Let's start with the stick."

"If you don't surrender, my guys start firing wildly at the dorms and we blame Other terrorists for the deaths."

"What? You're willing to kill innocent students for—"

"I'm willing to do a hell of lot more than that to get what I want," she spat. "So spare me your indignation and judgment. Whether you're capable of understanding this or not, I am fighting for the greater good. Besides, I still have the carrot."

Shit, she was one evil bitch, willing to kill innocents to get us to surrender. {{ISA NEEDS TO HAVE SOMETHING SHE WANTS}}. I have spent enough centuries with all sorts of evil to know when someone fully intended on backing up their threats. Serena would fire at the dorms. She would kill students to get us.

I thought back to what Seth had told me back at the O^3 house: that I would attract monsters. Well, he wasn't wrong—I'd just thought those monsters had claws instead of manicured nails.

Serena. The World Army. They were worse than just about every monster I'd faced; they were smart, ruthless and absolutely convinced of their own rightness.

"So, onto the carrot," Serena continued. "Egya."

Hearing his name was like a punch in the gut. "What about him?" I quivered, my heart racing at the possibility that he'd been captured. Or worse.

"He's off contacting the resistance. Stupid name, by the way."

"I know," I said, but as much as that was an open for a wee bit of banter, I was too distracted by what she had in store for Egya.

"Regardless. I will let him go."

"What?"

"I will let him go. And the changeling as well as that weird ghostly fellow. I will let them all go. Of course, none of them will ever know what happened to you, but—"

"And Isabella? What about her?"

There was a long pause before she said, "I can't let her go, but I promise you this: I will not kill her. I need her, but once I am done with her, I will release her. This I swear. This is my oath to you."

"Humans don't have many qualms about breaking oaths."

"I do," Serena said without hesitation. "There is no way for you to know that for certain, but I do. I really do. I will let them all go. I will even try to save Justin. But I need what Isabella has, and I need it now."

"Screw you," I spat.

Serena sighed before saying, "From one evil bitch to another—I will keep my oath. You can put on that human lie detector and have him hear my words."

I gestured for Mergen to come over and listen in. As soon as he was in earshot, Serena spoke. "I swear that should you surrender, I will let Mergen, Deirdre and Egya go. I will also hold Isabella captive, using her knowledge until the experiments I am working on are successful. Then I will let her go, too."

Mergen smacked his lips as he rubbed his belly. She was telling the truth.

"And what about me?"

THE HEAVIEST OF BURDENS

"Let me guess, you're going to throw me in some dark dungeon and—"

"I'm going to kill you," she said, as if stating some indifferent factoid like there are three hundred and thirty-six dimples in a golf ball, or two thousand, seven hundred and eighty-nine miles between New York City and LA. "It will be painless, but you will die. So there you have it. The truth."

I didn't need to look over at Mergen to know she was telling the truth.

"And let's not forget: do not surrender and I will kill innocent students. I will order my men to fire wildly at the dorms."

Mergen licked his lips. She was telling the truth.

"OK," I said, "I believe you. Give us a minute to consider our options."

"You have five. Then I give the order to shoot."

20
WE ARE ALL CHERUB

J grabbed Mergen's hand before walking over to the others. "You do not tell them what she said. You understand? We have to surrender, but Deirdre will never agree if she knows what's going to happen to me. Swear to me that you will never tell them what you heard." I paused, fighting back a tear. "Even after."

Mergen stared at me, his ghostly white eyes sullen and sad, but then he nodded. "I swear."

"Good," I said. "Then let's go tell them the good news."

Walking over, I put a hand on Deirdre's shoulder. "We're beat. We can't win this one. We fight, we lose. We run, well, even if we manage to get away, they'll find us. We are simply beat. We have to turn ourselves in."

Mergen rubbed his belly.

"What did Serena say?"

"Oh, a bunch of stuff. Mostly that if we turn ourselves in and hand over the anti-venom, she'll let Deirdre, Mergen and Egya go. She also promised not to hurt you, but she said you have knowledge she needs. Sounds like she's going to force you to work for her."

Isabella nodded slowly. "Not surprising. I did steal everything she knows about Others."

"She promises not to hurt you. She won't let you go either, though."

Mergen licked his fingers in agreement.

"And you, milady?"

"Dungeon," I said, giving Mergen my death stare to make sure he didn't expose my lie by making a face like he was sucking on a lemon or something.

"Then we will—"

"No Deirdre, we will not. She also promised to start killing students if we didn't surrender. I can't let innocents die because I wasn't willing to spend a little time in some cell. I just can't live with their blood on my hands. Not when I could have prevented it. No, my friend—my dear, dear friend. We have to surrender. Please."

"So what? We give up. What about Justin?" Isabella's panic was rising, and I was sure that everyone who didn't listen to my stay-in-your-room advice heard her.

"She promised to try and help him."

"But—"

"Isabella, we have no choice. Let's say we try to fight. The Gone-Gods know that with Deirdre here, we could make a good show of it. But they've got guns and all kinds of nasty projectile weapons. There are too many innocent kids here to risk it."

"But Justin," she said.

"He'll be fine," I lied. She knew it, Deirdre knew it ... and when Mergen's face went sour, any illusions I was trying to create were dispelled.

"OK, so he probably won't. But there's still Egya. He could help us."

"How? Once we give up, we'll be taken into the facilities and disappear," she said. "We have to fight."

"No," I said. "Sometimes we have to accept the hand dealt to us. I cannot ... will not risk anyone getting hurt for something we have no chance of winning. I'm sorry, but we turn ourselves in. That is the right thing to do."

GoneGodDamn it, I hated taking the moral high ground.

The demon in me wanted nothing more than to fight.

But the Cherub—the better part of me that was my father—demanded that we protect this place. And protecting it meant surrender.

I removed my mask and put my hands up in the air. "Come on, let's get this over with."

↔

Surrendering sucks.

It's not just that you have to admit defeat. It's not the humble pie you're forced to eat or even the bleak future of incarceration, torture and only the GoneGods know what else horrible tortures that face you.

It's knowing that with your surrender comes the end of hope. Hope for Justin, hope to stop the fifty shades of evil these guys were doing, hope for whatever future you wanted to help build.

That future was something—the *only* thing—that both the angel and demon within me agreed on … making this world a better place for humans and Others alike.

Don't get me wrong. I had no delusions of grandeur that I, wee ol' Katrina Darling, would be the sole architect of that future. But as I walked to meet my fate, my heart sank that I would no longer be a player on the board. That my contributions, no matter how small, would no longer be a part of that future.

The demon in me wanted to go out in a blaze of glory. One last stand that would end with sweet oblivion. At least I could go out fighting.

The angel in me chose surrender because she wasn't quite ready to give up hope. After all, I had escaped three dead gods and a former ex-archangel. What made human incarceration any different? There might be a chance to escape while they transported me to wherever before ending my life.

There were procedures, protocol to follow. I'd have a day—or at least a few hours—to figure something out.

But Serena Russo didn't strike me as the type of evil that would let me escape. She was going to take me somewhere private. Somewhere quiet. And put me down with an injection like an unwanted dog.

The only thing that surprised me about all this was that I wasn't scared.

Most Others were terrified of death, seeing its finality as the worst of all possible fates.

But I wasn't afraid.

Why? I don't know.

Maybe it was because I was once a human—a human who got to live three hundred years—and humans know they're going to die as children. Or maybe I simply was too naïve or stupid to be afraid.

Or maybe it was that I once witnessed my father and his impossible bravery as he faced his own death with a smile on his face, and ever since then I'd vowed I would do the same.

So that was exactly what I did.

Removing the mask as I walked down the hill, I smiled ... staring right at Serena Russo as I did.

"You know there is no escape," she said as her soldiers flanked us.

"I know."

"So why are you smiling?"

"For reasons you'll never understand."

"What I understand is that I win."

"You do," I said, and Mergen smacked his lips as if to emphasize my agreement.

"This ends with me winning." There was a tinge of desperation in her voice, as if she needed me to believe her. But it came off more like her trying to convince herself. She held out her hand to Isabella.

The encantado hesitated before fishing out the vial and handing it over to her. Serena gripped it like she was holding the elixir of life itself, and that's when it struck me why she was so desperate to get us. That vial of serum we stole for Justin ... it was for someone else.

It's for her son.

137

Serena looked between me and Isa. "You're doing the right thing, you know. You can't possible understand why, but it's the right thing."

"And everyone else dies?" Isa said. "What about the others who need the serum?"

Serena pursed her lips in answer.

"Happy?" I said.

"I am." Serena turned to Isabella. With a tone that resonated with unbridled anger, she growled, "And you. I wanted nothing more than to be your friend. To work together to make this GoneGod World better. But you have shown your true, traitorous form. You are going somewhere very dark and lonely. And your precious love, Justin? Well, let's just say I'm going to let our little experiments run their course, for better or worse."

Isabella groaned, but offered no reply.

"So I win," Russo repeated. And then her eyes flitted as she looked away as if in shame, as if she knew full well that she was playing the role of villain in this little story and said, more to herself than us, "I win and there will be no destiny, no intervention of the gods, no curse or magic to alter that. Cuff them."

Three soldiers approached me, and I braced myself for their inevitable manhandling ... when this godless world offered up a miracle.

A miracle in the form of an empty beer bottle.

↔

It seems that even without the gods, the divine wheel of Karma still turns. Something that became wholly (and holy) undeniable when an empty beer bottle flew from the window of Gardner Hall.

21

THE TRUTH BITES

he beer can didn't even hit anyone, instead falling limply by the foot of the soldier holding me down. He looked at it before stepping down on it hard, crushing it beneath his feet.

I couldn't help but smirk at this minor act of defiance. Someone took the risk of expressing their discontent. Sure, it wouldn't save me, but it was something. A minor act of bravery.

Only if everyone protested with minor acts of bravery ... then this GoneGod World would transform into something else.

But the thing about minor acts ... they were often gateways to bigger acts of bravery.

Bolder moves.

And that came in the form of a friggin' full beer can lobbed from a third-floor window of Gardener Hall. I looked up to see that some enterprising physics student was using exercise elastics and a couple bras to create an impromptu slingshot.

"Fire a warning shot and let's get out of here," Serena said.

A soldier standing at her side unholstered his pistol and aimed it in the air, but before he could fire off the shot, another beer can came flying, hitting him in the stomach.

He keeled over as three more cans came flying, and not just from

Gardner's windows—from all around. Molson, McConnell, even the back of Douglas Hall ... students, both Other and human, were lobbing full beer cans at the soldiers.

Minor acts and heavy burdens ... GoneGod fuckin' damn!

We didn't need to be told twice. Immediately getting to my feet, I slammed into the soldier nearest me.

Deirdre, as strong as she was, pulled apart her restraints and picked up two soldiers, tossing them like empty sacks against the wall of Douglas Hall.

"The psychics," I cried out to the changeling. "They're how they found us."

Deirdre didn't need to be told twice. She immediately went for them, knocking them both unconscious with a thud.

Now we could escape and couldn't be followed.

At least until they woke up. But given how hard she hit them, I figured we had a few hours at least.

I ran over to Isa and helped her to her feet. It was harder than you'd think, given that we were both bound. "Isa, transform. Get out of here. You know what you need to do. Go, now."

Isa looked at me and shook her head. "What about you?"

"I'll fight my way out and meet you where we said." GoneGods, I hoped she knew what I meant.

"But ..." Another beer can flew past her, hitting a soldier in the shoulder.

I heard the military van engine roar to life. They were retreating.

Or getting ready to pursue us should we run.

Either way, we needed to make our move. And now.

"Isa, I really appreciate this act of bravery, but we really don't have time for this. Go. Go now."

The encantado nodded before pursing her lips and transforming into Malik Unlike before, the transformation was instant. So all the times she slowly shifted in front of me was so that I could witness her power.

Show off.

An instant later she was bolting down the hill.

I turned to Deirdre and watched in awe as she dispatched four more soldiers, quite literally using the largest of the bunch as a club against the rest. "Deirdre," I yelled out, "put him down and follow Isa. Protect her."

"But milady," she said, still holding the poor soldier in her arms.

"Go!" I ordered. "I will follow. Promise."

Deirdre hesitated before dropping him to the ground. As soon as his body touched the earth, he crawled away for all his worth. I swear to the GoneGods he could have beaten an Olympic sprinter with that crawl.

The changeling fae nodded at me and followed Isa down the hill, bounding forward with such force that she must have cleared ten feet.

The soldier with the pistol tried to follow, but I managed to kick him in the back of the knees. He went down with a satisfying thump.

Now it was time for me to escape.

Might have done it, too, if Serena wasn't so damn smart.

I felt a pistol at the back of my head. "In the van. Now."

And as she forced me inside, I lamented making that promise to Deirdre. I hated having to break it.

I guess there was still a bit of Other in me after all.

↔

Mergen and I sat bound in the van. They had put us both in handcuffs that were, in turn, chained to the security van's narrow metal benches.

Serena sat across from us, gun in her hand. "Do you know what this is?" she asked. There was one more soldier—the one who had originally bound me—sitting next to her, his pistol aimed at my head.

"The part of the story where the villain reveals her dastardly plan?"

"No," she said. "Not at all." Serena banged on the van's wall and cried out. "Stop the van." Then, turning to the soldier, "Get out."

"But Dr. Russo," he protested, but one glare from her was all he needed as an answer. He got out without another word, and a second later we heard the unmistakable sound of the passenger-side door opening and slamming shut.

I guess he didn't like being so summarily dismissed.

"Don't like an audience when …" I nodded toward her gun.

"What? Oh, this …" She looked at the gun like it was the most foreign thing in the world. Like she'd never considered using it. Like she hated its precise nature.

"So what is this?" I asked. "The part of the story where you tell me your plan, try to win me over with some heartfelt rant? Or is this the part of the story where you threaten me and everyone I love?"

Serena chuckled, her gaze distant. "Oh no," she said. "You got this all wrong. This is the part of the story where I beg."

22

THE FINAL COUNTDOWN

"Beg?"

Serena looked down at her lap as she ran the palms of her hand against her suit pants. "You killed your father, didn't you?"

"No," I lied, to which Mergen grimaced like he'd just taken a bite out of a sour peach. Looking at him, I growled. "Hey, whose side are you on, anyway?"

Serena smirked. "He is an avatar of truth. He can no more help his reactions to lies than we can hide our own pain. It's his nature."

"Oh brother," I said, turning to Serena and giving her my best eye roll. "Don't you go all cliché on me and start talking about our natures and how we can't help but be who we are. And I swear to the Gone-Gods, if you tell me the parable of the scorpion and fox, I'll scream."

"Humph, no. Nothing so trite."

"OK, so I killed my father, what of it?" I said, steeling myself against the emotion that bubbled inside. Thinking of my father ... my dad ... it was the one thing that always threatened to bring out tears in me. His loss, and my role in it, are my greatest regrets.

My greatest shame.

But I was face to face with the villain, and I couldn't afford to show weakness. Not now. Not here.

Not if I had any chance of surviving this night.

She smirked at my flippant comment. She'd done her homework, and she knew that I was lying. She knew full well what kind of emotions evoking my father's memory did to me.

"What would you do to bring him back?" she asked.

Anything. The thought was so immediate, complete and fast that I couldn't stop myself from thinking it out loud. I simply couldn't.

Mergen smacked his lips and rubbed his stomach.

Serena just nodded.

I gritted my teeth, angry at myself for not being able to control my emotions. With a growl, I held Serena's gaze and growled, "If you offer me a way to bring him back—"

"Nothing like that," she said, her voice distant, matching her thousand-yard stare. "If I had that power, we wouldn't be here. But I do not have any power over death. Nothing like that."

I noticed Mergen getting fatter at that comment. I'd seen this before. Some truths meant so much to the person speaking that it hyper-nourished him. He got big, fast.

Serena's impotency over death wasn't just a true statement. It was something … *more* to her.

"Then what is this?" I asked.

"Do you know why I joined the World Army? Not because I give two shits about the plight of humanity or Others. I joined because I needed their resources. And their influence."

"Because …" I feigned boredom.

Because …" she sighed, removing her glasses. She looked tired. Almost beaten.

But she didn't need to finish her sentence. "Because of your son."

↔

Mergen burped. I mean, seriously dude … way to kill a moment.

But that was exactly what he did. He burped like he'd just had one of the most satisfying meals of his life.

It was so out of place … I mean, we were literally in a life-and-death struggle, and here he was acting like he'd just maxed out at some Michelin Star steak house.

Serena and I shared a laugh. Almost like we were friends. But that camaraderie was short lived, because as soon as the moment passed, her face went deadly serious. "How do you know about Collin?"

"For one thing, he's the password to your computer. But for another, I saw him through the window of your house."

Serena nearly stood, except the van's roof prevented her from doing so. Her face turned dangerous, a darkness passing across it that would have made me shiver if I still had it in me to be afraid of people like Serena Russo.

I knew that look on her face; that was the fierceness of a mother.

In this moment, she was a lioness.

"What the hell were you doing at my house?"

"Staged a little break-in, as you may recall. Don't worry—Collin was fine. He looked pretty excited by the whole deal, actually. Cute kid."

She stood over me like she would slap me—or maybe use that pistol after all. Her hand was shaking, the pistol's nose trembling.

And then, with a long exhale, she sat back down.

Actually, she slumped. And all the fire and fury seemed to fall away. "He's dying."

I swallowed. "Of what?"

Maybe she hadn't heard me, or maybe she'd ignored me. Either way, she continued like I hadn't spoken at all. "I tried to save him with the aqrabuamelu's venom, enhance him like I did the cadets. It worked at first, but he's falling apart. His body is literally crumbling before me and I can't do anything about it." Her eyes glistened with unescaped tears.

"So make more?"

She shook her head. "You saw the aqrabuamelu. He's gone. And without him, we're done."

"You're still draining him."

"Nerve agent. Seems those poison glands can be animated with a little electro-stimulus. Everything else is gone, including the part of him we need to produce more anti-venom."

Mergen licked his fingers.

"You shouldn't have killed the golden goose."

She nodded. "Don't lecture me. It was a mistake. A mistake made, and now cannot be reversed."

"Find another scorpion man," I said. "But you're not stupid. That mission is underway, isn't it?"

Again, Serena nodded. "Do you know how rare they are? He might have been the only one, and now he's gone."

So that was it. There was only so much anti-venom and no promise of making more. And what they did have she wanted for her son.

"What about Justin?" I asked.

She shook her head.

"So, let me get this straight. You're willing to sacrifice Justin, let him and the others die, to save your son."

"The other cadets already had the anti-venom. They are out of danger. It is only Justin and my son who are left."

"And you only have enough venom to cure one of them," I muttered.

"Yum," Mergen muttered. To give the Avatar of Truth his due credit, he did cover his mouth after he realized his faux pas.

"So there you have it," she said. "My son or Justin. That is the choice we have to make."

"Humm, let's see ... the son of an evil bitch or the man I love."

Mergen grimaced.

"Which part?" I asked him, but I knew the answer. It was all of it. Serena wasn't evil. Not completely. She was just trying to save her son. I'd do the same thing if I was in her position. And as for my loving Justin—it was time to call it. I loved the idea of him. But my heart … it didn't belong to him.

It never did.

Still, I couldn't sacrifice him for Serena's sake. That wasn't right, either.

"So," she said, "here's the part where I bribe and threaten you."

"Oh, I'm waiting with bated breath."

"Give me the venom and I'll let you all go. New identities, a fresh start. Or you can join us—"

"Why would I do something like—"

"I read your profile. I know who you are better than you know yourself," she said. "I know that you want nothing more than to take up the mantle you inherited from your father."

"What I want," I growled, "is to live a normal life like a normal girl."

Mergen grimaced.

"Shut up, Mergen," I spat. "You're not helping, and you're not always right."

To that, the Avatar of Truth was surprisingly neutral.

"He's right," Serena offered. "And so am I. You say you want a normal life, but yet you dress up like a Divine Cherub—for what? Because you're bored. They're not your problem, and yet you constantly make them your problem. You want to be your father's daughter. You want to make up for killing him, and you think becoming a Cherub will do exactly that."

Those last words did it for me. True or not, I'd heard enough. "And what about you? You want to save your son at what expense? The lives of others … all destroyed because of one little boy. How fucking selfish of you. How fucking—"

Serena stood. "I'd burn down the world to save him. Do you hear me? I'd kill everyone and everything if it meant fixing him. And that means you and your friends. Everyone you love. Everything you have. Give me the anti-venom or face my wrath."

Mergen groaned with satisfaction at her rage. And that was when I saw my chance.

I stood, too, my restraints not giving me full mobility, but still enough for me to move. "And I'd do whatever I can to stop you … and not because I love Justin, but because what you are doing is wrong. You want the truth. You want my truth … You're right. I don't want to be normal. I don't want to be human. I want to pick up my father's mantle. I want to become a Divine Cherub with the power and means to save the fucking world from assholes like you. But that's not the whole truth. There is one more piece to it…"

I let my words hang, holding Serena's gaze before I said the one thing that I had never admitted to anyone, myself most of all.

I screamed my deepest truth.

I screamed the one truth that meant more to me than anything else.

"I don't want to make up for killing my father. I want to become him. Become the good, selfless badass muthafu—"

That was all I needed to say, because as soon as those words came out of me, the van carriage burst open, freeing us.

Such is the power of my truth.

23

FACING OUR DEMONS

OK, my words didn't have the power to crack open the steel carriage, but the meal that Mergen was eating off them did.

Mergen ballooned up like the Michelin Man on steroids, at first pushing us against the steel walls. But Mergen knew what I was trying to do and had put his arm against the wall, bracing himself so that he could push the van wall.

Seemed the truth not only let him grow, it also made him stronger, too.

We popped out of that van as the tires burst under Mergen's increased weight.

Within seconds, I was outside, although I was still chained to the metal bench.

Good. After all, a metal bench could be used as a club.

A club I used against the soldier who was stupid enough to come after me.

Him down, I jumped onto Mergen's back (with the bench still awkwardly attached) and rode the giant avatar as he ran downtown. I must have looked like the blonde being kidnapped by some albino King Kong.

I turned just long enough to see Serena Russo's cold eyes glare at me as we ran away. Whatever humanity I'd seen in those eyes was gone, replaced by the hardness that comes from someone who will stop at nothing to complete her mission.

I could relate. Seems that Serena and I were cut from the same cloth.

Fine by me, I thought as I mirrored her cold stare.

↔

Helicopters filled the sky faster than I thought logistically possible. Seems Serena had them on standby for something like this.

She was the kind of person who had contingency after contingency, and such foresight made her more formidable than most beasts I'd faced before.

Mergen cradled me like some messed-up bride as he looked for the threshold he could lift me over to safety.

"OK, Mergen, I think we can do this. Head for the cross and—"

"No. Too many."

"So we keep running until we find an opening. Maybe if we head to a garage or—"

"Too many," he repeated, and I saw a look in his eye I'd seen too many times before. He was going to do something stupid. "Thank you, Katrina Darling, daughter of Eoughan MacMahon, friend of Mergen the once Avatar of Truth. You are his daughter. You are him. No more hiding from that truth. Promise me."

"That sounds a hell of lot like goodbye," I screamed.

He smacked his lips. "Promise me."

"Mergen—"

"Promise me," he repeated.

"Fine, I promise. Now you promise me … no hero shit," I yelled. "I need you to survive this. I need you to live."

Mergen's gaze trained on the sky as it filled with more and more helicopters, their spotlights shining on us.

"I need you to live," I repeated. "Please." We were passing the alley behind the McGill Bookstore. It was narrow, but also filled with huge garbage cans, big enough to hide my small frame.

I saw what he was about to do.

"I need you to live," I said, my eyes blurring with tears.

Mergen looked down at me with soft eyes as a sad smile painted his face. He yanked the bench free of me with one tug, leaving me with just the chain around my wrist.

Then he did something I didn't know he could. He lied. "I will," he said, as he jumped over the first cans, dropping me inside.

The can fell over and I helplessly watched as he continued to run, cradling his arms as if I were still in them. I watched, and in that moment I swore I would never hide from the truth again.

Ever.

↔

I waited until I could no longer hear the helicopters. From the sound of it, Mergen had lured them away from me, up the hill, toward the cross. I suspected it was by the cross that he planned to make his stand. The Avatar of Truth and warrior poet … he was going to fight them for as long as he could so that … what?

So that I could live.

I crawled out of the can, determined to make his sacrifice mean something.

↔

I broke into the bookstore and stole a McGill hoodie and wool hat. I looked like the poster child for the university. Not that I cared. It was cold and I needed to get to the others.

Making my way to McGill's Science Building, I was careful to avoid the main roads. The good thing about Montreal in the winter ... it was so cold that everyone walked like they were on a mission, head down and covered in bulky clothes.

I fit right in.

When I got close to the building, Egya, Isa and Deirdre appeared from the shadows. I fully expected Egya to start cackling and make some joke about college spirit or something, but instead he just hugged me, and I could sense the fear in him.

He was trembling. Actually trembling.

"Oh thank the GoneGods, girl. I thought you were done for. But then we heard reports about a giant white ghost rampaging through downtown and, well, here you are." He wiped away a tear.

"What's going on?" I asked, eyeing him carefully.

"Ahh, nothing," he said. "I was just worried." He tried to hide his eyes.

And that wouldn't do. Not one bit.

I grabbed his cheeks and did something I should have done a long, long time ago. I kissed him. Hard. In all my time here at McGill, Egya was the one person who truly understood me. Ex-immortal, ex-hunter ... he embraced his past and future in equal measure and tried to guide me to do the same.

He was my friend, but he was always more than that. He was the mirror I needed to see who I was.

And now I was starting to understand that. Understand myself ... and well, here we are.

At first he was taken aback by my move, almost pulling away, but as soon as he clued in that this wasn't a joke, but something for real, he leaned into the kiss, holding me tight.

By the GoneGods, he held me tight.

I don't know how long we embraced, but it must have been quite a while. "Ahem," I heard the encantado say. If the encantado, mistress of seduction and hopeless romantic was interrupting us, then I guessed we probably were carrying on a wee bit too long.

We pulled apart. "What was that?" Egya asked.

"Me finally accepting who I am and who I was," I answered.

Deirdre clapped, walking in close and saying, "I shall fell a mighty tree and build you both a yurt for your wedding. I will decorate it with—"

"We're not getting married," I said. "How about we date first?"

"I don't know. I kind of want a yurt," Egya said.

I rolled my eyes and looked up the mountain, where all the helicopters circled the cross. The battle between Mergen and the World Army had begun. He was a badass warrior. He'd hold them off for a while.

He was buying us time.

He was sacrificing himself so that we could stop them.

I turned to my Scooby Gang composed of a shapeshifter, a changeling and an ex-were hyena. "OK folks, it's time to get to work. We have an army to take down and only a few hours to get it done in."

24
KAT'S TO-DO LIST

*B*y now, stopping—or rather, killing—me was clearly number one on Serena's To-Do list.

That was fine, because we had a To-Do list, too –

1: Plant bombs around the World Army headquarters – CHECK,

2: Isa gets Serena's pass so we can infiltrate the facilities and then pretends to be me so Serena will chase after her – CHECK,

3: While that's going on, call in a very real bomb threat so that said facilities will be evacuated – CHECK,

4: Isa downloads any and all useful information – CHECK,

5: I find Justin – CHECK.

GoneGodDamn, I thought as Isa and I finally got into the room where Justin was resting, *we're doing it, ladies and gents.*

I rushed to Justin's side, pulling the IVs out of his arm. He groaned with an abandoned pain as the needles left him and almost immediately, the greenish tinge started to leave him.

"Justin," I said, shaking him.

He groaned, but didn't move.

"Justin, come on. Wake up."

Nothing.

Taking the syringe that Isa had prepared out of my bag, I started to inject him.

But before I could plunge it down, he woke. "What? What are you doing?"

"This is anti-venom, Justin. This will cure you."

"Is there more?"

I was taken aback by this. This was the absolutely last thing I expected to hear from this drugged, dying man.

"What did you say?" I asked, seeking to confirm what I thought I'd heard.

"I heard them speaking ... about how this is all there is. About who else needs it. Is there more of the anti-venom?"

I shook my head.

"Then give me half."

By now Isa was by his side. "No, you need it all. Half will—"

"Buy me time while we find a way. Half. Save half for the others."

So there it was. Justin was sacrificing himself and a guaranteed cure for the sake of others. I knew why I had loved him. A man whose soul was so pure that he'd face death for others ... that was a quality in short supply in the GoneGod World.

"Will half do it?" I asked Isa.

Isa's eyes fluttered as she muttered some calculations in her head. "Yes. He's right, it will buy him time by keeping the poison at bay. But it will eventually come back unless—"

"Unless you find a way." He took her hand in his. "And you will find a way."

Isa nodded, her resolve clear.

"And"—his eyes met mine—"burn this place to the ground."

I gave him a single nod. "On it."

He sighed and lowered his head.

"OK, so that's settled," I said, plunging the needle into his arm. I gave him a wee bit more than half, but still left enough behind for ... well, for Serena to do the right thing with it.

Then I left the vial for the evil, mad scientist to find.

I promised myself, in that moment, that I wouldn't tell Isa about Serena's son and how sick he was. There was no point to it. She didn't need to know why Serena was doing what she was doing—it was hard enough, given how much Isa loved Justin.

As soon as the green liquid entered his system, the scales started to flake off like someone had descaled a fish on his bed. His skin turned back to human flesh color as the green undertones that had previously painted his body faded away.

He was turning back to normal, just like Isa had promised he would.

You go girl.

"Excuse me?"

"Nothing," I muttered. "The serum is working, that's all."

"Good. That's very good." I heard her breathe a sigh of relief. "And it's taking its toll, too. Look. He's gone under again."

I gave Justin a shake. Nothing. He was out, and from the way he didn't respond to me, I could tell he'd be out for a while. "No," I yelled back.

"Makes sense. It will be hours until the serum makes it way through his body. He will be asleep for some time."

Looking at his limp body, I groaned. No way we could carry him out of here. He was simply too big.

But what's the expression: when the GoneGods don't give you the physical strength you need, they give you four wheels.

Something like that.

Nothing's ever easy, I thought, unlocking the hospital bed wheels. *Looks like I'm going to have to cart you out of here.*

"Did you say something?" Isa called from the other room.

"Nothing—just thinking out loud," I called back as I started to push the bed out of the room. Where was Egya? Once he got here, he'd be strong enough to lift Justin.

Under the rush of clicking keystrokes, she giggled. "Yeah, you do that."

Another rush of clicks as I pushed the bed out of the restricted room and Isa was up on her feet, holding a flash drive in her hand.

OK, so that went smoothly.

The far door clicked open and Russo entered, a look of utter shock crossing her face when she saw us.

Smooth like sandpaper.

↔

"Isa, what are you doing?" Serena asked. "Your oath."

Isa shook her head. "You broke your promise to me, Serena. You are not trying to make this world better. You are not trying to unite us. You are trying to destroy us."

"No, that's not true. Our mission ... *my* mission is to heal—"

"Put a lid on it, lady. The gig is up." Hey, I know it's antiquated tough-guy talk, but when you've lived through the era, you still get to use it.

"You!" She pointed a finger at me. "You are the cause of all this."

I did a curtsy, circa 1800s-Scotland style.

"Don't you see? We're trying to fix things. Make things better." Her eyes fixated on the flash drive in Isa's hand. "And I cannot let you leave with that."

Isa cupped the flash drive in her hands, and a soft glow emanated from them. When she opened her hands, the flash drive was gone. Best magic trick ever. Except it wasn't a magic trick. It was just magic.

"The information is part of me now, along with all my other research. You'll have to kill me if you want to stop me from having it."

"Neat trick, girl," I said, channeling my inner Egya.

Russo shook her head with mounting frustration. She grabbed the phone on the wall. "Security. I need you in Main Room 1, now."

"Not to ruin your already totally ruined day, but no one is coming to help you. This place has been evacuated."

"What? Why?"

"Protocol. That's what you do when something is about to go

boom," I said. "Turns out that making explosives is way easier than you'd think. Especially if you have a scientist like Isa here. So unless you think you can take on an encantado with a mean right hook and an ex-vampire with a dirk, I suggest you run."

I could see the wheels turning in Russo's head as she assessed the situation. She was sunk. The facility was going, and there was no way she could stop us alone.

A single tear rolled down her cheek as she realized that her life's work was about to be destroyed. That her *one mission* was about to be lost for all time.

I sensed genuine pain in her, and I almost felt sorry for her.

Then Justin moaned, and any empathy I had for her evaporated with that moan.

"You don't know what you've done to me," she said. "To my family."

"The cadets were never your family," I said. "They were just kids that you took advantage of … That you used." I pointed at the vial sitting on the counter. "Look, we even left half for you. Not like you'll use it on the cadets, will you, Russo?"

Isa seemed confused, but said nothing.

Russo shot me a look of hate so sharp it could have felled a Red Cedar. She grabbed the vial of remaining anti-venom off the counter —enough, probably, to keep her son going for a little while. "You are a menace, and this GoneGod World will be better off without you."

"Tough words for an unarmed scientist standing alone."

"Oh, my dear Kat, I may be unarmed, but I am never alone." She took two large steps toward one of the consoles and typed a string of letters. With her last stroke, the second Restricted Area doors opened, and the largest centaur I'd ever seen came trotting out.

So the rest of our To-Do list went like this:

6: Inject Justin with anti-venom – CHECK,

7: Escape – OK, this last one was proving to be quite difficult—and finally,

8: Live.

As I stared at the fire breathing, berserker centaur blocking our path, I was beginning to doubt the possibility of that.

The centaur looked at me, and I expected him to say something or yell. But instead he roared.

And with that roar, he breathed fire.

Oh joy.

25

THE HEAVIEST BURDEN

Run, Kat. Run.

I had to lure the centaur away from the others so they could escape—which was exactly what Serena was doing right now.

As soon as she'd unleashed the centaur, she booked it out of there. Which was, after all, the right choice: we only had a few minutes before the whole place went boom.

No biggie.

I spun on the encantado. "Get Justin out of here. I'll take care of My Little Pony."

"But—" Isa began.

"No time," I growled, turning back to the centaur. "Hey, big guy. Want some oats?"

That worked like a charm. The centaur charged at me, its massive hooves seeking to crush me under their considerable weight.

When I'd faced the centaur in the club, I had sought to get under him and delivered a well-placed shot to his underbelly—a centaur's Achilles heel—but this centaur was bred for battle. Genetically engineered, actually—and just like the other one, his underbelly was also covered with dragon scales stronger than steel armor.

THE HEAVIEST OF BURDENS

Plus he was fast. Don't get me wrong, centaurs were normally fast, but this guy speed boarded on supernatural.

I dodged another swift kick and, running into the main room and jumping over a few rows of computer terminals, made my way to center stage like I was entering an arena or something.

Not that this area was designed as an arena. It was the central hub to the control room with several doors leading deeper and deeper into this modern dungeon.

To my right was the room where Justin was being held. And behind me was the room where that poor aqrabuamelu was being drained.

And for dramatic effect, I put on my father's mask, adorning my mantle as the Divine Cherub. I honestly didn't know if I'd win this one, but if this was to be my last fight, then let it be while wearing the mask of the man I loved most, while fulfilling my purpose, embracing it once and for all.

Egya would be proud.

I gave the centaur a Bruce Lee-style taunt as I prepared myself for the coming battle. I didn't have to wait long; the centaur leapt over the terminals with a single bound, and from his fiery mouth he spat lava-hot spittle at me.

As in, literally.

I dodged the spittle and watched in horror as the ground lit up under its heat. "What the hell did these guys do to you?"

It wasn't a legitimate question ... I really wanted to know.

Whatever it was, they did something similar to Justin and only the GoneGods knew how many more.

I pointed my dirk at him, waiting for his next attack, taking comfort that in a few minutes this place would go up in flames and burn all the messed-uppedness of this place.

And that Isa, unimpeded by Serena or anyone else, would escape to wherever Egya had arranged for them to go. They would live a life on the run, but at least they'd live.

"Serena was playing god when she made you. Zeus would not

approve," I said as the centaur looked down at me. Evidently he was planning his attack, seeing that a furious lunge was something I could dodge. In other words, he was getting smart. More calculating.

And deadlier.

"Zeus and his pathetic cohort are gone. We have only this, and I am more powerful than I ever was. More complete." He stretched out his chest and beat his gong-like hands against it. "If he were here now, I would challenge him for the right to rule."

Over the past six months I had met wannabe gods ... hell, even met a few dead ones. This guy didn't come close to their power. But he had their ego.

And that was something I could use.

"Really?" I said. "More like you'd pull his carriage."

The centaur brayed in anger.

"Nah, pulling his carriage is too good for you. More like act like his pack animal. You know, carry his luggage or—"

That did it. The centaur reared onto his hind legs before charging forward with the full force of his being. As he charged, he shimmied left and right, evidently trying to anticipate which direction I would tumble in my effort to dodge him.

But I didn't dodge him. I let him charge at me, and timing my jump as perfectly as I could, I leapt up onto his chest and pivoted onto his shoulders, where I covered his eyes with the palms of my hands like some demented game of peek-a-boo.

The centaur reached up for me, grabbing me with both his hands, but I was small and on his back. He did manage to pull off my father's mask, not that it mattered. I didn't need the mask to do what came next.

As he fumbled to throw me off him, he didn't pay attention to where he was going and crashed into the holding pen where the aqrabuamelu's husked-out body was still being pumped for the last of his venom.

The last of his venom ...

As soon as the centaur crashed into his body, I pulled at the restraint that held the aqrabuamelu's tail and plunged it into the centaur's neck.

The centaur pulled back, but it was too late. Enough venom went into him and he started to fumble as the powerful being's poison shut down his nervous system and stopped his heart.

The centaur died faster than I expected, and in his death throes he pulled so hard on the arachnid's tail that he ripped it clear off at the joint.

Traces of the aqrabuamelu's acidic blood spewed out of him. I guess being dead didn't mean his blood was gone.

And his blood burned like acid.

I know because splashes of the burning liquid hit my neck and cheeks.

I felt my skin dissolve in the most hideous, horrific pain I've ever experienced in my three hundred years. And trust me: I've experienced some hellish pain as both a human and a vampire.

Through the agony, I knew I had only a few seconds to neutralize the acid or it would burn its way through my skull. Luckily, I had been in this room before.

Well, Isa had ... and I had been right with her, watching carefully through the camera on her lapel.

I saw where everything was kept ... including where a base agent was stored.

Smashing my elbow through the glass casing, I pulled out the liquid and poured it over my face. I felt the acid neutralize and knew that I wasn't in danger of dying.

But my tongue also felt the absence of flesh, finding its way out of my mouth even though my lips were sealed.

There wasn't enough foundation and blush in the world to cover this scar.

Not that it mattered. All that mattered now was that I got out of here.

This place was going to explode in a matter of minutes and, hideously burned or not, I needed to get out of here.

↔

I ran through the empty halls of this place, retracing my steps as I did so. During the fight, I had lost track of time. I had no idea how many minutes were left until the explosives went off.

Did I have two more minutes?

One?

No idea.

Also, I may have stopped the acid from burning into my skull, but it still burned. A lot. Parts of my face were missing, it felt like my head was in flames and I was starting to blackout from the pain.

Hold on, Kat. Don't stop now.

Up the stairs and down the hall, back through the security door we had met Isa at … and then down two more corridors, up one more flight of stairs and I'd be outside.

I made my way through what felt like Minos' Labyrinth, expecting the ground to light up with every step I took. Thankful that every time my foot touched the floor, my world didn't ignite in flames. All I could think as I ran was, *Step, no boom.*

Step, no boom.

Step, no boom.

I had to keep going. No matter how much I wanted to stop, lay down and never get back up again, I couldn't. If I had a shot at life—disfigured as I might be—I would take it.

I was at the final stairwell where, at the top, I saw both Egya and Deirdre waiting for me.

Egya with his semi-transformed face and Deirdre with her lush blond hair and youthful cheeks.

But neither of them were happy when they saw me.

Egya wasn't smiling. Instead, he had a look of absolute horror on his face.

Why? I had made it. I was almost outside.

But almost wasn't enough.

I took one more step, and then I felt it. The first of the explosives going off.

Step. Boom.

The stairwell crumbled, and I felt the sensation of falling just before my world went dark.

And in that moment, I died.

26

THE LONG RIDE HOME

I'd like to tell you that there is some light at the end of the tunnel or that your loved ones are there to meet you. I'd like to say that angels are playing harpsichords as the pearly gates open before you.

I'd like to tell you that something ... anything happens.

But the truth is that all I saw in that moment was darkness.

Darkness and peace.

Then I felt what can only be described as being struck by lightning as the world suddenly came into view again.

And the pain returned. So much pain.

Deirdre and Isa stood over me. Deirdre's face had aged and her flawless blond hair had strands of gray as her tears rode along the crevasse of her newly-formed crow's feet that sprouted from the corners of her eyes.

An IV was in my arms as Isa stood over me like the healer that she was, her careful hands guiding me back to life.

My face hurt, my chest hurt. Every part of me was in pain.

And then I saw Egya, his eyes bloodshot with tears and worry. He pushed aside the other two, kneeling close to me, his hand in mine.

"Is she ...?" he asked.

"I'm …" I started, but my voice wouldn't come.

"Will she …?" he repeated.

Isa checked my vitals again and nodded. "She will be fine. In time." Isa looked down at me with pity in her eyes. Like she wasn't staring at the me, me … but something else.

Something less.

"What?" I said, but I knew where that pity came from. My cheek had been burned with acid; my looks had been taken from me.

I'm not ashamed to say that part of me wished I had died back there, rather than live as this scarred human being.

The shallow part of me.

The rest of me was glad to be alive. There was so much more work to do.

I touched my cheeks and forced a smile. "This. Haven't you heard, ladies … this is the latest fashion accessory. Scarred a la acid." I tried to force a snotty French accent, but everything hurt too much to pull it off.

"I can burn more time—" Deirdre started.

"No. You have done enough."

"But my pledge to you. My life for yours. Always." She put a fist on her chest. The fae salute.

"No …" I said, taking her hand in mine. "Our lives for each other."

I tried to sit up, but couldn't. I was strapped down. "Where? Where are we?" Then I saw the metal, brown ceiling and knew exactly where we were. In the van I had 'bought' from the tattooed guy after Isa infiltrated the World Army facility.

I looked to the side and saw Justin hunched over in the corner. Asleep.

So he had made it, too. Good. *He'll be on the run, but he'll be with Isa.*

That was worth something.

And as for myself … well, I laughed (on the inside; on the outside I couldn't even really move my face). But my chest constricted with my laughter, little exhalations leaving my chest.

I couldn't help myself.

I laughed as I looked at the three concerned faces that looked down at me as if I had just died (well, I guess I did).

"What ...? What's so funny?" Egya said, his own lips parting with a slight smile.

"I was thinking about how we're on the run now. And how much fight there is left. And then I thought about Scooby Doo and their van —the Mystery Machine. I always wanted my own Scooby van. And crew. Careful what you wish for, eh?"

Careful, indeed.

↔

The next three days were a whirlwind of insanity. Serena didn't let up, employing all the resources of the World Army to find us. But try as she might, word had gotten out about what happened.

About what we had stopped.

That bought us a lot of good will ... not only with Others, but some of the more moderate humans as well. They hid us and, if not that, lied on our behalf. At any given moment, we—me, Egya, Isa, Justin, Deirdre—were spotted in a hundred different locations all at once.

Eventually the search died down enough for us to part ways.

We found our way to Justin's Mustang, and in the dead of night sent Isa and the boy with the impossibly beautiful eyes and thick lush hair on their way.

Egya had found the resistance in New York City, and they had promised to help them.

I knew they would ... Isa was far too valuable to let fall into the hands of the World Army.

I would love to say that there was some grand goodbye. That I stood next to them and gave them some rousing speech about burdens and carrying the heaviest of weights.

That's what my father would have done.

But I was still reeling from my scarred face.

And in my pain and self-pity, I watched them leave from a window of the Scooby van.

There was one moment, though. A single moment when Justin turned to the van and saluted me in the manner common to the old Scots. It was something I had told him about long ago, in one of the rare moments when I spoke to him about my father and how the other Divine Cherubs would always hold such high reverence for him.

They always saluted him with the highest respect. Ridged postures and proud eyes. That was how they always were with him.

Seeing that while lurking in the shadows as the monster I was, the monster they hunted, always filled me with pride for my father, shame and envy for myself.

I, too, wished to know what it felt like to have such respect.

Justin gave that to me. He did so with the generosity that was so common of the first human I ever loved.

↔

With Isa and Justin gone, it was time for the rest of us to start … but I didn't know what we were supposed to start.

Start fighting?

Hiding?

Running?

Organizing?

I had no idea. And my uncertainty filled me with a dread that consumed my recently returned soul.

The only constant I had was Egya. The boy from Ghana loved me. He loved me despite my hideously scarred face.

He loved me despite my turmoiled soul.

But his love wasn't an answer to what came next. That was something I needed to find for myself.

And I did.

The answer—well, *an* answer of sorts—came to me a few days later when the three of us were holed up in a cheap hotel on the outskirts of Montreal.

Zoolander played on the motel's cheap, bulbous TV, and Egya was trying to explain why it was funny to Deirdre. The changeling warrior couldn't grasp it and the irony of how similar Deirdre was to *Zoolander* hadn't escaped Egya and me.

That night I laughed. Laughed until it hurt.

Wiping away tears of joy, I went into the bathroom to reapply my running mascara (funny how I still applied makeup to my face, like I was still the same dainty girl I had been only weeks ago).

In the reflection of that motel mirror, I saw who I was.

Who I am …

Not a cutesy ex-vampire, but something more *evolved*.

And in that instant, I understood that although I didn't know what the future held for me, it didn't matter. What mattered was that I keep striving.

Keep trying.

Keep evolving …

And as I stared in the mirror at my burnt face, I saw that both Egya and Deirdre now stood behind me. *Fuck it. Whatever tomorrow holds, at least I won't face it alone.*

In answer to my thoughts, Deirdre slammed her fist against her chest.

And as for the boy with the annoying cackle and beautiful smile. Well, he simply nodded, bowing low before saying, "No girl … no you won't."

THE END … sort of.

Hey there, Ramy Vance here and I'd like to thank you for reading…

. . .

I'd also like to get real with you for a minute. The GoneGod World is an ongoing world with tons of adventures yet to be had. We've only completed PHASE 1 and part of PHASE 2. Lots more to come, but I need your help.

Writing in the GoneGod World is expensive and with a young family in tow (my 2-year old Bunny Banshee and my 6-year old Monkey Face), I need to make sure that I pouring in my time into things that help secure their future.

That said, my non-Urban Fantasy stuff sells better... but my heart is in the GONEGOD WORLD.

I want to see this world to it's bitter end. I want to wrap up PHASE 2 and get tucked into PHASE 3 where Kat will return in a spectacular way... but I can only get there with your help.

The good news is your help should be fun. (I hope, says the author with a gulp.)

I only need 2 things for you:

Share the stories with friends, family, the barista at Starbucks ... and anyone else who listens. I give you full permission to be annoying as hell.

AND

Keep reading!

Speaking of 'keep reading':

THE GONEGOD WORLD CONTINUES: Check out our other series ... same world, different hero!

ALSO BY RAMY VANCE

Mortality Bites Series

Mortality Bites

Family Matters

Superhero Me!

Orphaned Follies

Dawn of a Thousand Sunsets

Three Dead Gods

Run, Kat, Run

Encantado Dreams

The Heaviest of Burdens

Looking for a great deal? Grab these book bundles...

Setting Fires with Dragons - complete series

Mortality Bound - complete series

GoneGod World - Complete series

Series Starter - Bundle

ALSO BY RAMY VANCE

Mortality Bites Series

Mortality Bites

Family Matters

Superhero Me!

Orphaned Follies

Dawn of a Thousand Sunsets

Three Dead Gods

Run, Kat, Run

Encantado Dreams

The Heaviest of Burdens

Shattered Vows

GoneGod World Series

GoneGod World

Keep Evolving

CrystalDreams

Penemue's Inferno

Looking for a great deal? Grab these book bundles...

Setting Fires with Dragons - complete series

Mortality Bites - complete series

Mortality Bound - Complete series

Series Starter - Bundle